BONDS OF MIDNIGHT

JANUSHI RAICHURA

Made with ♥ on the Notion Press Platform
www.notionpress.com

For Hetansh, for being my most patient unpaid therapist and listening to me cry about the same guy a hundred times without judging me,
And for saying the wise words,
"But sometimes...not wanting to have regrets is what makes you execute actions which make you regret...everything."
This one's for you, Mr. I am vengeance, I am night

Contents

It'd been three months since she had felt the sun touch her skin. The bracelet around her wrist felt more like a lock, a shackle tying her to the darkness of the Prince. She held firmly the invitation to the Winter Carnival of Ganea, her *home*.

Her chambers were lit lightly by some glehlium flowers native to Sleyisea Empire, but even in the dimness, she could easily see the plea in her mother's writing to come back home. She brought the parchment closer to her nose, hoping to get some remote sense of her mother, but all she could smell was tears and the regular scent of Ganea's papers.

Even then, some sort of comfort and *courage* sank into her, making her rise from her rocking chair. She caste a look at the quilt she had made earlier for the Prince to give something to smooth the impact of her request.

Eliana had spent her life living in fairytales. Her Kingdom was like a fantasy story: it always smelled like fresh rain and flowers, and that was the biggest speciality of Ganea. The fields stretched everywhere around them endlessly with no disease plaguing their lands and no enemies strong enough to wage a war.

Her sister Roese used to whisper tales from different kingdoms in her ear everytime her parents weren't there. Often, she made some stories up to keep Eliana entertained during events. She would take her down to a well every Friday and would wish for a handsome prince and then ask Eliana to make a wish herself. Eliana was loyal enough to wish for the same thing, the same gift her sister wanted.

Everyone knew the wishes never came true, that the goblins stole the gold people caste in to the well and it was just a ploy to be rich.

But people hoped, because that was what Ganea was; a land of hope.

And those lingering feelings made Eliana hope that perhaps the Prince wouldn't be as mad as she'd imaged and perhaps he would let her go back.

She picked the quilt; it was shimmering silver just like the Prince's hair, just like the Prince liked it. Two guards followed her closely as she headed for the Prince's chambers with two maids behind her.

The Prince's guards entered the room to inform the Prince of her arrival, to return moments later with the door open. The guards followed her inside with two maids: one carrying her coat and another quilt.

Eliana was certaom that the Prince's chambers were the most beautiful part of the castle. Everything around her was pure black in color with golden and silver designs. Platinium-white flames danced around the room making the embroidery shine bright than it usually would.

His chambers were like a house. The main room had velvet black sofas on one end and a balcony on the other. She had never entered his bed chambers, but had glimpsed enough of his study to know for sure that it was marvelous.

A chandelier hung high in the middle of the room with crystals casting lights all around. The flames were quiet that day, making the crystals create star-light projections on the jet black room.

Sleyisean empire was infamously known as the Night Kingdom because of the creatures that lurked in the dark. Creatures like the Prince. Eliana had never actually explored the kingdom, it was too high of a risk for a royal to take. Her dresses were brought to her room for choosing and her guards always accompanied her every time she was required to make an appearance with a Prince outside the castle.

But from all the churches she'd been to: both holy and unholy, she knew if she had to choose, the Prince's room would be her favourite place to worship.

A guard opened the door to the balcony and she realized that the Prince was out enjoying the cool breeze. A black hooded coat was draped over her shoulders and head by a maid. It was a light silk coat that went perfectly with the red dress her designer Eloise had picked out the morning but it did nothing to give her warmth against the winds roaring outside.

Nonetheless, the joy of standing out under the enchanting night sky drew a hum of appreciation out of her. A few feet away from her, the moon shone on the silver mass on the Prince's head. She took a tentative step in his direction making him turn towards her.

Something happened to her heart. She wasn't sure what it was, but it started beating rapidly in her ears. She was yet reminded again that he was the most beautiful creature she could ever lay her eyes on. He was dressed in an untied black vest and black pants. His shirt underneath was unbuttoned halfway to reveal his chest. His hair was up ruffled by the winds and his eyes were hazy clouds of grey and silver. He held a glass of blood firmly in his hand.

He wasn't like the night, he *was* the night.

"How may I help you, *princess*?" the title came out as a mock-*as an insult*. She had married him and had become a princess of Sleyisea from Ganea, but without their marriage fulfilled, it was as if she was the princess of both the lands and neither of them at the same time. He set aside his glass on a table and folded his arms, looking at her with a complacent smile on his face.

"I made you a quilt," she uttered, and the maid presented it to him. His eyes merely took it in before he gestured to set it on the same table as the glass of blood.

"I am certain you aren't here just to give me a quilt, Eliana," his words came out smoothly, easily, as he watched her intently, making her squirm.

She gulped but replied truthfully, "There's a fest in Ganea. There hasn't been one for seven years since..." her voice trailed off as memories sunk in her head. "I would like to go, if that's not too much to ask for,"

The words hung in the air until his eyes darkened and ran over her body before coming back to her face.

He took a heavy step in her direction, and his smile turned more smug as he asked, "And what will I get in return for letting you go?" she could all but whimper at the question as his eyes darkened. His eyes held a fog in them that made her stare for a minute too long.

A beat passed, and she could see his fangs extend forward and could feel her heart palpate in her ears. The balcony opened loudly behind them, and a lady in a thin white chemise entered. "Your Highnesses," she dipped into a curtsy that displayed her entire cleavage, her eyes playfully flickering to Alex as if to see whether he was watching her. Alex's eyes darkened further and Alex gave Eliana a tentative look that sounded remotely like an apology but the hunger in his eyes was obtrusive. "You can go to Ganea," the dismissiveness in his voice was concealed firmly but she could sense it nevertheless. She picked up her skirt, turned around and walked out of the room just when the girl's moans started covering the night.

The rest of the day-*night* passed well for her. Jealousy stung a little, but it was nothing a little red wine couldn't solve. She was content with the Prince's answer, but time and time again, flashbacks of his gaze crawled up making her shiver-sometimes with fear and sometimes with something a little darker.

The maids had packed an order of twenty-two dresses for her: six for the daytime activities of the fest, six for the nighttime shows and ten for travel. Apart from that, she had several chemise and robes and bathing salts, candles, and some blades.

Each dress took up a separate big wooden box for carrying. It had everything: a coat, separate jewellery and footwear. But she only had the boxes. Her designer had refused to show her the dresses. She had seen the itenery of the event and had designed a different dress herself for each activity. She had sent an inquiry at the shops to order the materials for the dresses and the jewels. Eliana was aware that she was trying to get the work done at a short notice, but Eloise was only determined.

Eloise got her measurements like she did every week just to be sure nothing had changed but it always did. "You have lost weight again, Princess, have you not been eating properly?" she asked, scrunching her brows in a way she always did while thinking of designs. Eliana knew that even as she asked the question, her mind was elsewhere, trying to figure out a way to make her look radiant.

"I have been eating properly!" Even as she said it, she knew it was of no use. She had that argument with people on daily basis and was used to it.

"If you lose another inch by the end of the event, one of your dresses is going to fall right off you body!" with that, she called for her maid and asked her to make her eat extra during dinner.

It was about four in the morning when she was finally done signing all the requests for the jewels and money and the maids drew her a bath to get her to relax. She usually had baths after dinner, but the stress had her worked up too much. The maids pulled her in a lace black nightgown. Her nightgowns and inners were the only pieces of clothing that she owned that weren't red.

The maids pulled a similar black robe over her gown as a maid came to ask her presence for the dinner. Eliana's circardian rhythm was messed up because of the Prince. While everyone slept, she stayed awake and because of that, she and the Prince had started having dinner together.

It was the only time they actually met or had a conversation. He was usually immersed in reading even during the dinner, perhaps to avoid conversation or the awkwardness, and apart from that, they never crossed paths despite their chambers being adjacent.

Eliana had half a mind to skip dinner because of how weary she felt from the day's work, yet Eloise's words kept on ringing in her head as a warning. "I would like to have dinner in my chambers tonight," she informed her maid who scurried away to get the message to the Prince and another left to get her food.

Her chambers were almost as big as the Prince's, and she had all the accommodates that he did. The maids readied her dining table and pulled out the crockery from the cabinets. A minute later, she was seated in a red velvet chair with the maids serving her food.

A knock came on the door of the room. She heard it open and a guard appeared in front of her and he said, "The Prince insists that you join him for the dinner."

The guard's tone was stern and final. Eliana sighed, rose and followed him to the Prince's chambers. He was already seated at the head of the table, and was already immersed in reading when she entered.

He didn't look up, not even as she walked towards him, took off her robe, and took a seat beside him. From the corner off his eyes, he eyed a guard and said, "Leave us be," the maids quickly served her and scurried off outside along with the guards.

Silence reigned with nothing but the sounds of the spoons and dishes clicking against each other to fill it. "You asked for me?" she questioned, praying that he hadn't called her to cancel the trip to Ganea.

He didn't respond, instead he questioned back, "Any particular reason I am having the misfortune of having my wife shame me by walking around in her lingerie?"

Her face heated at those words. She'd hoped that his eyes would darken like they did when that girl arrived, she'd hoped he'd notice her and desire her, but he had chosen to not even look at her. "I am sorry. I had a long day. I was too tired to dress back up,"

"Tired from emptying my kingdom's treasury, I see," Her neck curved downwards as the insult sunk in. "If I ask for your presence for something, you cannot deny it, or need I remind you that I am your Prince?"

"Pardon me, Your Highness," a chilly gush of wind reminded her of how little she was wearing. She grabbed her robe and put it back on, fastening the belt as tight as she could, to cover as much as possible. She suddenly felt too vulnerable in the attire. Perhaps it wasn't the best thing to wear in front of a vampire Prince.

From the corner of her eye, she saw the Prince do something and the windows shut themselves. But it did nothing to make her feel better. "You don't seem so good," the Prince spoke, his eyes dropping from her face as if to assess her thoroughly. "Have you lost weight, Keizer?"

A hint of concern remained evident in the question but it remained hidden behind the mocking use of her maiden name. "A little," she mumbled, her eyes on the caviar in front of her.

Thankfully, he didn't pressure her to speak further. The cold kept on rising deeper inside her body, making her shiver uncontrollably.

"I would like to retire to my chambers, if you don't mind, Your Highness," he gave a mere nod in response, his eyes not leaving the pages of his book. He rose to his feet and extended a hand towards her, putting his book away.

Hesistantly, she took it and he walked her quietly to the room. The guards kept a distance as they followed, but she knew that with the Prince there, she didn't need those guards.

But the Prince isn't going to protect you. A voice whispered in her head.

"Your heart just slowed down," the Prince muttered, opening the door to her room. His eyes took in the room behind her as he held the door. He'd never really visited it after she'd had it renovated.

"Do you want to come in?" she asked, biting her lip. His eyes dropped to the floor for a second and he ran his hand through his hair before answering.

"I have work," with that brisk reply, he closed the door and she heard his receding footsteps. He'd been that cold since forever. There was no reason for him to change. A part of her had hoped he'd come in and treat her the way a husband treated a wife. She'd hoped that for once he wouldn't have treated her like one of his Sleyisean subjects, but he hadn't wanted their union, just as she hadn't wanted it.

A knock on the door woke her up the next day. A maid opened the door and returned carrying a basket filled with fruits and several plates with bread, omelette, and meat.

"What is all this?" she questioned, rubbing her eyes sleepily while rising from the bed.

"The Prince had this all sent for you, Your Highness," a guard informed from the door. Eliana grabbed her robe and tied it up as she checked out all the food the Prince had sent.

"Prince Alexander?" Eliana questioned just to be certain. The guard nodded before turning back around and a maid closed the door behind him.

"Put the food through the tasters!" Eva, the head maid instructed a chambermaid.

"That's fine. The Prince has sent it, there's no need to put it through the tasters!" Eva looked at me for a moment before asking the some chambermaids to serve the food on the table while instructing the other to draw Eliana a bath.

Eloise had a gown ready with jewellery in her closet by the time Eliana was done with the bath. It was a simple strapless red dress with a sweetheart neckline and a red rose at the side in the middle. It came a little below her knees up front and touched the floor at the back.

A maid did her hair while another helped her put on the jewellery before she had breakfast.

After finishing her food, she checked on the paperwork sent back by the Prince of Night, approving all her requests for the jewels and the money. She smiled to herself...even if the Prince didn't love her, he wasn't setting a limit on her spending.

"It's time for your archery classes, Princess," The Night Kingdom was very strict on training their royals how to survive the toughest of situations. Elianor had been learning how to fight since her second day in the land. They'd have her three hours out in the field learning something or the other. Somedays it was archery, some day sword fighting, some day throwing knife and a long list of other things.

She was always informed in advance, or at least her designer was so that she could pick out a dress that didn't stop her from fighting that way.

Archery had never been her strongest suit, and it had only gotten worse when her training hours fell under the moon rather than the brightness of the sun. And the worst thing was that people expected her to have her husband's night vision.

Targets awaited her in the field, stretching in a wide range. The grounds were empty apart from her maids, guards and her tutor, Sir Kalon. He stood in the middle of the field, awaiting her with his hands behind his back.

The crest of Sleyisea was on his red tunic, embedded in golden. He was almost thirty-five, and had been tutoring her since she had changed her sleeping schedule. "Your Highness," he gave a short bow before turning to a guard and saying, "Take a bow and a quiver fit for the Princess," he tilted his head to a bunch of bows and quivers of different sizes.

A maid slipped gloves on her hands. Over it, a thumb ring was put on by another maid along with finger tabs. A bracer was put on the inside of her left arms.

The knight instructed her to get a grip on the bow, and just as usual, asked her to set the arrow on her target. Thing was, there were no torches lit, no sources of light. The moon barely formed a crescent behind the trees.

She knew she was supposed to shoot, she just didn't know where. She aimed recklessly at something in distance, hoping it was where she was supposed to shoot, making the knight say, "Your Highness, pardon me, but do you intend on killing that poor maid in distance?"

She instantly lowered her bow and turned to him frustrated, repeating for the hundredth time, "I can't see in the dark! I am not a vampire!"

"Nor am I, Your Highness. You don't see me making such excuses,"

"You have practice! I don't-"

"We are *getting* you practice, Eliana!"

"*Princess* Eliana!" a sharp voice came from the behind. Eliana dropped her bow in surprise while Sir Kalon drew his sword as they both turned in the direction of the voice. There, holding a goblet filled with blood, stood the Prince dressed yet again in black with his hair swept to his side. Sir Kalon dropped to his knee and the Prince smirked, questioning, "May I have the pleasure of teaching my wife?"

CHAPTER TWO

"Of course, Your Highness,"

The Prince turned in her direction and she gave him a small curtsy before speaking, "Good Evening, Your Highness,"

He ignored her completely and addressed the knight when he spoke again, "You made her wear satin gloves, it is as if you *want* her to miss her target!" his voice remained contained, but rugged enough to scare the knight.

"Pardon me, Prince Alex, I thought they'd protect Her Highness's hands from any damage caused by the bowstring!"

"She's not made of paper, Kalon. Take off your gloves and all of that as well," he instructed and she obeyed without hesitation.

"Your Grace, she could scar her hands-"

"I suppose that's my problem, isn't it. We don't need your supervision, Kalon, you may leave now," flustered, the knight left throwing Eliana a pitiful look. She lowered her head, her eyes fixated on the ground. "Leave us," she knew that was for the maids and the guards from the way they scattered away the next second.

He picked up another bow and a single arrow for her and handed it to her. "Thank you, Your Highness,"

"I think we've reached a point where you can address me by my real name, Eliana," she'd always felt her name was ordinary until she had heard him say it. It rang with such passion and possessiveness that it almost didn't sound like it belonged to her.

Something gave her the courage to raise her head and stare into his eyes. He handed her the bow and the arrow and came up right behind her.

"On battlefield you won't have time to put on your armours or even your gloves. The enemy won't wait for your to be ready. Learn to tolerate some pain, *princess*," And there it was, the mock again.

"Yes, *Your Highness*,"

He ignored her attitude and spoke, "Take a minute to take in your surroundings. Let your eyes adjust to the dark. And if you still can't see, we can always turn you into a vampire,"

She turned around so fast that the string of the bow strapped and attacked her right in the face. The Prince moved almost just as fast, but he couldn't save the string from getting embedded in her skin.

She sucked her torn lip to keep herself from crying out in pain as the Prince cursed. He quickly detached the string from the bow.

"Hold tight, my robin," with only those words as warning, he scooped her up in his arms and ran to her room faster than humanly possible.

She somehow managed to keep herself from crying as the tears only made it sting more. A healer arrived a few minutes later followed by her helpers carrying all sorts of remedies. She closed her eyes and her hands formed fists around the sheets as the healer started applying the ointments.

By the time the healer was done patching up her wounds, Eliana was covered in blood. It slid down her neck and stained her gown's neckline, all the while soaking her hair. Her eyes met with the Prince's and something darkened in them and she realized she was bleeding in front of a vampire.

The Prince rose up from the chair as soon as the healer left. "I need to finish some work," he spoke quietly, his eyes drifting anywhere but towards her.

He turned around but before he could take a step, she asked, "If I asked you to stay, would you?"

He lowered his head, sighed, and then walked out of the door as if she hadn't spoken at all.

That morning she dreamed of the last festival of Ganea.

Flowers overlooked the entire garden beds, stretching for miles in distance. They had a good harvest that year, with just the right amount of rain and bouts of sunshine. Ganea had magic seeping through its veins, through its rivers and the air that everyone breathed.

It was a land of the pagans.

Nature always shined upon them, with mother earth's gifts splurging from the crops. Pagans were the followers of nature itself, with abilities that surpassed all of the other magical beings. Nature answered them every time they called out to it.

As the younest princess of Ganea, she was showered with gifts from people all over their land. The first day of the festival was dedicated to that: the people showing their love to the royals.

The King and the Queen sat in the centre, with the Princesses by the Queen's side and the Crown Prince by the King's side. One by one, families came forward, rewarding gifts to a royal or royals of their choice. Eliana's brother Cade received by far the largest number of gifts, enough to make both Eliana and Roese jealous.

People served him swords and knives and arrows. Some brought forward tunics, while some stuck to special magical items blessed with curses.

Their father gained the allegiance of men and excited little boys. Old women gifted him food items while younger woman shyly offered some stitched works of their own. Their mother received the most boring gifts out of them all. Most people gave her a part of their harvest: it was a variety of crops but nothing much. Some brought her dresses while some logs and coal for the hearth.

Roese got a wide range of white dresses. She was sixteen, and her marriage was something the entire land was looking forward to. Their were different veils and undying flowers with the finest of jewelley. Many lords and knights and messengers of a few princes brought with themselves a proposal.

And Eliana got the prettiest of tiaras, some beautiful dresses, unique stones, a pony, loads of flowers, a chess board, a bow with a bunch of arrows, a tea set, a variety of dolls and jewellery and toys, and a single proposal, one from the Night Kingdom.

It wasn't ideal. The Night Kingdom wasn't the best of a land. It was powerful and vast, it's army was unbeatable but it wasn't the best place to send your daughter, at least that was what the advisors told them.

The royals didn't make much of a proposal, no one even bothered opening it and reading it. The King, their father, believed that she could do much better, and her brother promised that he would let her marry out of love when he ascended the throne.

Roese's proposals were put aside and assessed thoroughly that night by the advisors while the performers started a show for the royals. Not everyone paid with gifts, some decided to showcase their talent.

The jester had already once gone through their programmes and supervised their work, just to be certain it was safe for the royals.

The night had started with fireworks. The local folk had performed a dance, the elders had sung. A circus from the nearby town had performed followed by jousting and melee and the night yet again experienced some fireworks.

Eliana woke up feeling homesick for those experiences and almost forgot about the cut down her face and the previous night's event crashed on to her, dampening her mood.

A hollow filled her chest as she remembered that he had left.

She'd asked him to stay, not really because she needed him but because she wanted to see if he'd stay.

But he hadn't.

Eloise told her that they could hide the wound until it had at least clotted. It was impossible, but that was what she needed; a scar to form.

"A scar like that would take years to disappear even with magic. The Prince must've done it on purpose so no one could steal his beautiful wife," a chilling sincerity laid behind her joking words.

"It wasn't his fault,"

"Bowstrings don't snap by themselves. He could've done it and you wouldn't have even realized. He's a vampire, my darling,"

They didn't go further into the conversation. Eloise picked out a dress for her and left with that, leaving her alone with her thoughts. She knew Alex hadn't hurt her on purpose. She'd known him for seven years, and even though he didn't love her, he somewhat cared for her, she knew that for a fact.

She knew that because even that day a basket came for her with food. It was again bigger than it should be, but she hadn't been able to have dinner the previous night, and the Prince hadn't underestimated her hunger.

By the time she was done, only a bite of chicken was left. "Do the Prince and I have different cooks?" she asked her chambermaid while she was cleaning the table.

"No, Your Highness. But I have heard that for the past two days he has been getting breakfast from elsewhere just for you." A smile came to her face before she even realized.

That night, the Prince came yet again to her chambers.

She stood in the doorway while he ran a feather-like finger over her bandage and asked, "Does it hurt?"

"I have suffered worse," she replied, unsure whether to be honest.

"Not what I asked," his hand dropped to her shoulders and he guided her outside gently. He let go of her as they entered the grounds.

"Are we doing archery again today?"

"Yes. I spoke with Kalon. You were good at almost everything else. I suppose as a parting gift I should help you out with archery," he handed her a new bow. "I had the strings tested beforehand just to be sure."

"Thanks," she gingerly took it from his hands. He noticed her hesitation and his voice softened,

"I am sorry for what happened yesterday,"

"It wasn't your fault. I don't want your apology or your pity, whatever it was,"

Something playful flickered in his eyes and he dropped an arm around her waist and pulled her in his arms. She would've been mad if she hadn't been shocked and flustered by his gesture.

"You are mad at me," he leaned down to rest his head against her shoulder and pulled her closer until her back was pressed tightly again his chest.

"Alex-"

"So now you decide to use my name," he joked, turning her head towards him with a finger. "I am sorry, my dear robin,"

He kissed a side of her head and ran another finger on her bandage. "Don't worry, I am fine,"

"I have booked a safe passage to Ganea," he said all of a sudden. "I cannot come because of the treaty but I have called a hundred guards to take you there and all of your staff. I have yet to confirm the entry of the guards with the King of Ganea but they won't be representing Sleyisea. They're your personal mercenaries, paid for a month and till then, they'll only represent you. I have explained that in a letter to your father,"

"When did you get the time to get all that done?"

"Vampires don't need much sleep, my darling robin,"

She threw her arms around his neck and kissed him on the cheek. It was an impulsive gesture, something she had never done before. "Thank you so much for this,"

As gently as he could, he pried her hands off himself and turned her around. "Let's get back to shooting,"

Trying not to feel rejected, she trained her eyes back on the target and let the arrow fly.

The Prince had to carry her back to his room for dinner after they'd both realized that her pain medication had started to make her dizzy and that she was bound to pass out after an hour of shooting.

"I carry you one day and you make a habit out of it,"

"Stop complaining, you're a vampire, none of this affects you anyhow. Plus, Sir Kalon sort of mollycoddled me. I am spoiled, deal with it. You were the one who kicked him out,"

"Kalon carried you?" he asked, his voice lowering.

"Sometimes. And when I asked him really sweetly, he even helped me freshen up and get into my night clothes,"

"Not funny, robin," but the amusement was evident in his eyes. The ride to his room seemed so long somehow that she fell asleep right in his arms.

When she woke up, she was on the table with her dinner served in front of her. "Eat," the Prince ordered.

"I just want to sleep," she argued, but even as she said it, she felt her stomach grumble with hunger. She hadn't eaten since lunch and the medicines were making her hungry as a wolf. After eating, she passed out again on the table.

When she woke up, she was lying on the Prince's bed under the covers. He was lying right beside her on the blankets, fully awake, his head in a book. "Good you're awake, now I can have my bed back."

She shot upright on her bed, letting the blankets fall down, only to find herself in a thin underdress. "What-what happened? Did we-"

"Don't panic, robin, nothing happened. You fell asleep at the table. Your maids got you out of your dress and I put you to bed. That's it," she exhaled in relief before falling back down. Alex raised a hand and the lights dimmed in the room.

She saw him put down her book and lie down beside her. "Thanks for letting me stay," she whispered and he leaned towards her and kissed her forehead. "Are you cold?" she questioned, raising the edge of the blanket.

Tentatively, he got under the blanket keeping a safe distance between the two of them. She was touched by how much he took her comfort into consideration but spoke nothing about it.

She'd spent nights previously in his room; her wedding night and a week or so when she was *injured*.

He had taken care of her then as well, wordlessly so, as if they weren't the prince and princess-consort of Sleyisea and just two normal people.

She gave in to the darkness looming around the corner, and as it possessed her very conscious, it whispered in her mind that she had given in a long time back.

The second day of the festival was even grand than the first one, because it was a gift from the royals and the lords to the public. The people of Ganea led a happy life, and there was rarely a shortage of food, because from almost all the revenue collected, it was redistributed among the poorer of the people.

The lords sparred in the arena, while the ladies knitted up high on the mountains. *Fairytale*. That was what Ganea really was. A world from books Roese used to sneak into her rooms after midnight and read them till she fell asleep.

She had a lot of nannies but no one took care of her better than her own sister. And that was what she loved the most about Roese. In the world of royals where even mothers were often jealous of their daughters, such love between sisters was uncommon.

She was too young to notice all that, it was just what had always happened around them, but Roese was smarter, rebellious. She fought with her parents when Eliana obeyed like a pet fairy. Roese was fierce, she was a dragon, she was the most suitable ruler of Ganea, if not by age, then by courage.

On the morning of the second day, their mother, Candice, had woken the two of them by delivering some exciting news for them. Twenty-six marriage proposals had come for Roese, and seven of them were from future monarchs, and one of them was from the young Prince of Keovalan Empire, Daniel.

Daniel's coronation was in two months, and he had to find a suitable bride by then to at least have as a fiancé. According to Candice, the proposals were sent to several many princesses and some ladies.

Roese did not match Eliana's enthusiasm, as she stomped her foot and left the room. Candice sighed and made Eliana promise that she wouldn't act the same way as her sister did.

Breakfast was early, with only the five of them at the table. "I don't wish to get married, father!"

"You're almost sixteen, my dear Roese, you must start considering suitors! This is the best proposal you could've asked for. He's barely twenty-one. So young and the heir to such a powerful kingdom! You'll be a Queen, my darling,"

My sister sighed. "He won't love me,"

"Of course he will. Your father loves me," my mother prompted, but her father only nodded to that sentence.

"You can't marry a man with an inferior status. Besides, Keovalan is an empire of heretics. Your pagan powers will be worshipped there. *You* will be worshipped there."

"I don't want to be worshipped," Roese whispered, her head hung in defeat for she knew there was no convincing her father otherwise. Her only hope was the Prince of Keovalan finding another bride before they mailed back their conditions.

That day, lunch and dinner were all complimentary to the people of Ganea. An informal court was established, with the Queen leading it while the King drank away in peace with the nobles.

People approached the Queen with simple demands: some wanted seeds, some food, while some merely wanted to cry at her feet and kiss them for all the help royals had provided.

The jester performed some tricks that night. Both the princesses danced around to lively music with the daughters of some nobles.

The Prince sparred with the sons of the nobles and the soldiers using wooden swords. A few knights gathered to perform an act and alas, the King rose, asked for the Queen's hand and they danced away into applause and peace as the dawn sank.

CHAPTER THREE

Eliana had always dreamed of waking up in her husband's arms with her head against his chest, but that was all before she'd actually met her husband. The Prince wasn't awful, he was just different, so she was shocked when she woke up and found herself in his arms.

He had his one arm snaked around her waist, and the other was in her hair, carefully stroking some strands.

There was no heart beating under his chest, but she was certain hers was beating rapidly. "Good evening," he muttered, his voice deep and husky.

She turned her eyes up to look at him without tilting her head to find that he was already looking at her eyes.

Vampires were known to be cursed creatures, but in reality they bore a singular curse and enjoyed hundreds of gifts, one of them being beauty, that seemed to magnify tenfolds in the natural light where the sun didn't brush against the Prince's skin, but casted enough light in the room to make him glow like a god.

All his sinfulness seemed to vanish under the light where he looked no sort of the ravaging beast that he was. The late evening hues made him look more of an angel, the creature Eliana wondered if he once was.

She couldn't help herself-couldn't stop the urge to tangle her fingers in his silver hair that looked almost golden in the sunlight and he didn't stop her. "Would you be so kind and get the blinds, my little robin?" he asked as a sheet of clouds blocking the sun moved with the winds, exposing the room to the morning sun.

Eliana nodded before moving to her feet with practised agility that she'd taken years to develop, and walked to the window only to realize that she was in nothing but a thin white underdress.

She pulled the curtains while muttering reassurances to herself.

He's your husband.

He most certainly was, but that wasn't the only thing he was. He was a vampire with less sanity and more unsatiable lust for blood. He was stronger: he could kill her, ravish her, drain her entirely of blood, all at his will.

She was no match against his immortal strength.

She turned around to find another consolation for herself, to tell herself that he wasn't looking and hence, he couldn't be thinking of ways to hurt her. Instead, she found his eyes clung to her frame as if ready to capture every moment, every flicker of emotion going through her, and she was certain she had seen her previous thoughts on her face, for his face had hardened.

He reached for a black robe hanging on a chair to his side and all but threw it at her. "Leave," came out his command in a cold, ruthless tone, and just like that, their perfect little illusion was shattered.

Flustered, Eliana pulled the robe over her petite frame while trying not to let the shame and embarrassment show over her face. She dipped her head and walked herself to the door which unlocked by itself and opened as well.

She didn't need to have someone to tell her that it was Alex to know it was him. However, she didn't turn around, she walked straight up to her room, not throwing back a single glance even as she heard him rise and felt his gaze the entire journey from his room to hers. It hauntingly followed her, leaving aftermath strong enough to burn her back even hours later at the mere thought of it.

Night passed with ease, starting with Eloise forcing Eliana to try dress after dress and match it with the jewellery and ending with her quietly reading a romance novel on her bed. She had no sort of hardships in her life, but she couldn't help but yearn for all the love she'd read about the female leads in her books have.

No life was perfect except the ones that were fictional. She had learned that the hard way, and even though the Prince didn't love her, he had been nothing short of kind towards her.

Nevertheless, his kindness seemed to have a limit, because that night, she wasn't taken to him for her training. Instead, she was brought to another night, Sir Devlin, her previous mentor.

Finding him standing on the ground, one of the only friends she'd made in the past seven years, she couldn't help but fling her arms around him. He reciprocated it almost immediately, but she sensed the hesitation in his body.

She heard a throat clear behind her, making her freeze in her place. The sound was familiar: it was strong with a touch of royalty at the edges and power dripping from it. She dipped into a curtsy before even turning around, knowing very well who stood behind him. "Your Majesty,"

"Rise, Princess," came the voice of the young king Thaddeus. Thaddeus was one of the kindest rulers she had ever come across, yet he remained the most authorative one. She had learned to bow in his presence and be the princess the kingdom needed her to be if only to please the king. "Sir Kalon was proving to be troublesome, so I arranged for Sir Devlin to mentor you again, and by the looks of it, you seem pleased with the decision," his eyebrows were raised in the last line, making Eliana baffle for a moment.

She quickly composed herself and lowered her gaze to her feet before answering, "Pardon me, Your Grace, I was merely overjoyed to meet an old acquintance,"

"I'll only offer you one warning, Princess, vampires are highly possessive creatures. And they are skilled murderers,"

Eliana's breathing hitched at his words and she could barely manage to sink herself in a small curtsy yet again, this time for showing submission. Thaddeus was right, Alexander might never love her, but she was still his wife, and he would never let her seek out another man's company.

Even if he hadn't been a vampire, he wouldn't have let her. Things didn't work that way in her world. He was a prince and he had a reputation to uphold. The princess with another man- that too of an inferior status, wouldn't look too good for the kingdom. The Prince would not only kill Devlin, but also herself as a punishment, and everything would fall apart for Ganea.

The treaty- her marriage with the Prince, was the only thing keeping Sleyisea from unleashing. If she were to dishonour the Prince and the kingdom in that way, the King wouldn't hesitate before executing her, and he would even have a reason to do for, one that would only bring shame to her family, if not war.

Therefore, Eliana put another foot of distance between herself at Devlin at the underlying threat. She couldn't afford to let her family get hurt because of her recklessness.

At the same moment, a sudden shift in a nearby bush and a feminine shriek- not filled with fear but shock and pleasure, caught her attention. At once, she swirled around in the direction of the noises and grabbed her sword, unafraid of any beast who could be lurking in there.

Sir Devlin let his huge body cover hers as he unsheathed his own sword. Carefully gliding it in the direction of the commotion, he let the tip breach through the net formed by the leaves and with one swish to reveal empty space. Staring at the rows of trees standing guard for the creature, Devlin made a small jerk of his head before asking, "Care for some hands on training, Your Highness?"

Eliana nodded, and just to be sure, turned back around, only to find the King gone, whether due to fear or boredom, she knew not. She silently followed Devlin to behind the palace's garden that looked no less than a forest at the late hour.

She kept a firm grip on her sword and let her senses rise to the surface. The clouds spoke to her, carefully guiding her north, while the winds gave her a motherly advice,

Don't go.

But Eliana had to look. She knew she would never feel safe if there was a beast prowling around reading to kill her at any moment.

Veering Devlin towards the north, Eliana took the lead of their small quest. They'd only made it halfway inside the garden, when they noticed drops of blood on the floor, as if the predator was running away with the prey in his hold.

They immediately quickened their footsteps, ready to follow the beast to the depths of hell if needed, but before they could find it, a howl ripped the night's serene apart and made them pause.

The howl had come from the opposite direction, and had perhaps nothing with the being they were hunting, but only a fool would ignore such a call of alarm. The single howl indicated a lone wolf, and in Sleyisea, lone wolves only meant rebels, and no rebel would disclose his own self until it had won.

"The King!" Sir Devlin yelped as the realization dawned upon him. Perhaps, the King hadn't disappeared on his own accord.

"The King has his guards. Keep moving, Sir," Eliana commanded in a firm, yet soft voice that was the only thing at that moment that kept her attached to the side of her that was married to a prince.

"This could be a distraction, Your Highness, and the King's life could be in jeapordy!"

"Or that howl could be the distraction, Devlin. Keep moving," No, she was no longer a princess. She was a huntress with an unsatiable hunger and a horrible feeling crawling in her gut. She was going to find the monster and end him.

A gasp cut through the air on their right, and they stumbled towards the sound without another thought, and the sight almost made her collapse.

In front of her laid the body of a maid of hers, Ella with blood gushing out of wounds on her neck. The upper half of her dress was drenched completely in blood that seeped down to the edge of her skirt.

The sight made her lunch lurch back out, but she forced her food down because she realized one thing: the work was of none other than the creatures that fed on blood.

A vampire had murdered her chambermaid.

She didn't realize when she fell backwards, fortunately landing right into the arms of Sir Devlin, and blacked out.

When she regained her consciousness, she was yet again in the dark chambers of the Prince. She could hear his voice before she could conjure up the ability to open her eyes.

She could sense his fingers hovering over her body, the near touch burning into her flesh, forcing her to remain still. She didn't want to lose the feeling the fingers brought along with them, but she was curious. As they say, curiosity killed the cat.

Slowly, she let her eyelids rise up, and it took her a few blinks, but she adjusted herself fairly quick to the lights, probably because they weren't that bright in the first place. The Prince's hovering hand was gone, and the fire was replaced by ice. Cold, hard ice that matched the level of intensity but not the passion.

His gaze seemed to sear through the air and burn through her skin. He was angry, she could tell from the way storm raged in his brilliant white eyes. There was a hint of concern lingering behind, but apart from that, there was only rage.

"What happened?" she managed to form the question in pants. She felt the heaving of her chest, and the lack of oxygen crawling in her head. Alex's eyes snapped from her face to her chest, which chose to rise and fall with an unimaginable intensity. His expression changed for a wicked moment before he reached out a hand in her direction.

He leaned forward and rested his hand on her shoulder, slowly jerking it upward before letting his hand creep in the space between her back and the bed. His other hand curled around her throat and balanced her body in the position as the other hand tore the dress from behind.

Eliana's eyes widened at the act and a small gasp escaped her lips when he pressed his hand flat against an open spot on her back. Her wide eyes turned to look into his, and the action caused his grip to loosen on her neck.

She instantly fell back on his palm to trap the cool radiating from his body. he was almost as cold as death itself, but there was something about his touch that seemed to quiet her blood.

He turned his grip tight yet again and lifted her head off the bed along with half of her upper body. His hand on her back went lower and his fingers danced on the bindings of her corset before he tugged on them, hard.

A whimper left her mouth before she could control it, and the Prince's eyes darkened before he let go of his hold on her throat and let her fall back and sink further into his grip.

Oxygen flew into her lungs making her moan in the sudden relief, and she realized that he had done it to simply open up her corset so she could breath. Unlike the previous day, her maids hadn't undressed her, so, being in a corset in her condition had restricted her air flow.

Yet, he made no attempt to retrieve his hand. Instead, he let his hand crawl on his skin and go deeper until he reached her waist. He grabbed it under her dress, and she whimpered again when his cold fingers came in contact with her ribs.

He leaned until his mouth was mere inches from hers, and just when she thought he was going to kiss her, he brought his other hand to grab her head and lowered on her neck.

She felt her pulse flutter, and he seemed to feel it as well, because he pressed his lips right over her pulse point, tugging on her skin with his lips first before switching to his teeth.

Another whimper.

His teeth didn't cause any sort of pain. His ghost of a bite didn't hurt her, but instead, they made her jerk against him in surprise.

From the chair, he slipped on to the bed and took his position beside her, all the while not letting her out of his hands. He let go of her head only to pull her into his lap.

Another whimper, this time accompanied with a word. "Alex…" His name on her tongue seemed to pull him out of it. And he rose to his quick in a beat of a heart, letting her roll off her lap and fall on the floor.

She winced as her body hit the hard ground, but didn't complain, and Alex offered no apology. He simply pulled his coat closer before stepping over her body and heading to the door. "Your Highness!" Eva gasped from the door leading to the other rooms of the Prince's chambers as the Prince leaves it, and rushes to her aid. "Are you quite alright?" she asked, grabbing her shoulder to help her get to her feet. rise

"I am fine, Eva, thank you," she answered, trying not to focus on the pain ripping her body and her soul. She would've been dead if she had as much as let mere seconds pass with his mouth on her neck. He would've sucked her dry and would've left her for dead if she hadn't called out his name when she had.

But his loss of control around her didn't make her feel bad, instead she finally felt some sort of worth, a kind of approval she didn't know she craved until she felt his teeth on her neck.

Alexander had never in the past seven years tried to touch her more than necessary, and he most certainly had never tried to rip open her throat for him. In all the stories she had read, vampires were said to be uncontrollable beasts who feasted on the blood of innocents, especially young maidens, but Alexander, had never as much as laid a hand on her, much less try to drain her of blood.

Until that day, when he had abandoned her on the floor with every intent of sucking her dry. Eliana wasn't angry about it- she liked the fact even though it took her seven years, she had an effect on the Prince. However, she was nowhere close to being ready to face him.

Someone had killed her chambermaid, and intriguingly, the Prince was one of the very few vampires allowed on the castle grounds.

CHAPTER FOUR

Eliana had discovered something about the Prince that no one had in the past six hundred years of his life, that she was certain of. The Prince, while being known as a cold-blooded brute had a soft spot for young girls. While girls a little older happened to be his favourite meal, girls her age or younger were his weakness.

Eliana had read somewhere that the Prince once had a little sister, who had disappeared mysteriously when she was only twelve. She knew that it was perhaps because of that reason that he was so overprotective of little girls, but she had no complaints, because if he wasn't the caring man that he was, he would've killed her three days into their engagement.

On the last day of the fest, the people and the rulers of Ganea worshipped the gods of the pagans. Pagans were known to be the followers of nature, so, every god who was related anyhow to nature was technically said to be a god of pagans, even though, pagans only worshipped a few of them.

One of them was Jason, the main entity they worshipped. Jason, the god of pagans, was known to be everything nature defied. He was conniving, manipulative and smart, and had a thing for taking things that weren't his.

There was a ritual in Ganea where the Queen danced and drank wine all night on the last day of the fest to call out Jason. He came, but never early. He waited till the Queen was tired and every inch of her was aching until he finally made his appearance and gifted the people of Ganea with a good harvest the following year.

And just like that, he appeared in the last fest of Ganea. Yet, every peasant and every knight and all witnessing his descent from what was supposed to be heaven, knew there was something wrong.

The first hour passed by with little drama, but the tension sizzling in the air didn't cool down in the least. The second hour had only begun when two new gods descended from heaven.

The Queen of Ganea rushed to offer them wine, which they declined with a slight shake before turning to face the god of pagans.

One of those gods was Didhur, the god of revenge and the other was Lobium, the god of destiny, and also, the king of gods. Their mere presence shook the soft core of Ganea, and terrorized all the wide-eyed innocents residing in the land. They were known to be ruthless, and the three of them together was no good omen. Something was off, Eliana could tell so despite only being nine at that time. It was evident in the way Didhur strode over to where Jason was standing and grabbed him by his throat. Jason, the psychopathic, reckless lord, for the first time in Eliana's life, appeared afraid.

Eliana tried to run forward to stop them, she wasn't going to let them bully her god, but Roese held her back firmly. She was older, and certainly had a better understanding of a situation, and from the pained expression o her face, Eliana could tell that Roese knew where it was heading. Everyone seemed to know.

"How dare you touch her?" Didhur asked, the fine tip of his sceptor pointed at Jason's neck.

"Touch who, Cecily?" he questioned back, trying to look as playful and twisted as possible but the fear in his eyes was unmissable. The scepter's blade dug into his skin, drawing god-blood that trailed down his body and the drops ended up on the ground. The soil hissed at the contact with the foreing heavenly substance and all the dancers surrounding the throne of Jason took a step back.

Lobium marched in their direction, wind howling at his every step. Only then did Eliana notice the darkened clouds and the thunder raging in the sky. Even in the dark night, she could see the unnecessarily dark grey hue of the clouds that made her still.

"I curse you, Jason, the god of pagans," Lobium roared. "I curse you and all your people! Your magic will cease, and you shall all be doomed for the next rain and the one after that!"

All of a sudden, the ground slithered below their feet and Roese caught Eliana before she could stumble forward, but the two of them ended up on the ground anyways, however, Roese managed to hold Eliana before she could come to any sort of harm, just as Alexander always did.

People were considered lucky when they had one protector, Eliana had two, both who swapped roles when Eliana was swapped between the two of them. Alexander treated her better than most royals treated their wives, and Roese cared for her more than her own mother.

Alexander had never been close to her, but he had never remained absent either. When she was young and new to Sleyisea, he would walk her around the gardens in the evening after she'd have her dinner every week. He took her to lakes and to valleys beside the palace. He taught her how to hold a brush and paint and arranged tutors to continue teaching her when he was away. She never really enjoyed or understood art, but for the sole reason of the close proximity she gained by dabbling in it, she continued and pretended to love it.

It didn't take Alex long to realize how much she loathed it, and he instantly helped her switch to singing. She immediately fell in love with it, and he liked to tease her by telling her that if he ever wanted to find her, he could simply just follow her humming.

The maids often told her that she brought the castle back to life, and some told her that they found the Prince lurking around at times during her practice. The thought of him being outside the door with his ear pressed against the wall made her want to sing her best, which she did, every morning for six years, even as circumstances pushed them apart and created an invisible wall between the two of them.

She sang, and he always came to listen, even if for a minute, and even when she changed her sleeping schedule and began rehearsing at night. Their marriage only existed on paper, they were distant and he was nothing but cold. The only connection they felt was when she sang her heart out and he listened on the other side.

Alexander was nothing short of a romantic on the front. In the court or at events, ladies, some even married, lined up to have as much as a glance of him. Some were bold enough to come up front and strike a conversation with him, and some were powerful enough to flirt with him even in Eliana's presence.

He was kind enough to not lead them on in front of her, but not gracious enough to let them slide out. Eliana often found them leaving his room in the morning with a flushed face and hazy eyes.

Some days it hurt, but after a while, she got accustomed to it. She was aware that he owed her nothing, and she couldn't offer herself to him, she wasn't ready yet, but he was hundred of years old and he had his needs, she couldn't stop him with nothing.

She was left with nothing but dreams of what her life could've been if she had been one of the princesses out of the books Roese used to read her, yet whenever she fell asleep, she thanked the gods for giving her such a patient and kind husband, until the day she couldn't fall asleep knowing he resided in the room adjacent to hers, and was capable of murder.

That morning, she resisted sleep as much as she possibly could, and it wasn't hard. The fear kept her up till afternoon and then tea did its magic until dinner, which she didn't even have to force herself to skip for her sleep.

She was woken up too early for her liking by one of the maids. The sky outside showed no hint of light except the faraway stars, the magical entities who never failed to capture every movement of her world.

She found Eva leaning over her, whispering something, but only incoherent words fell against her ears. She felt the door of her room bang against the adjacent wall as an unearthly presence casted itself into the room. She watch as the fear in Eva's eyes magnified and she stepped back, turned around and bowed to the other person before running outside.

"Keizer?" the voice called out, making her still on the bed. The adrenaline forced the daze out of her mind and she jolted upright at the sound. Cold winds hit her square, making her realize that she was in nothing but a thin dark blue chemise that covered too little. She let herself fall back and pulled up the sheets till her shoulders to hide her exposed body.

Eery grey eyes bore holes in the sheets and for a hot second, she found herself wondering whether he could see through the silk. In a torturous pace, they slide up to her face, forcing her to hold in a gasp of shock.

In his unbuttoned grey tunic and black pants, the Prince looked no less than a god. His eyes looked hypnotising in the dim golden lights of the glehlium flowers, but with a glass of blood in his hands, she failed to focus on his beauty. She couldn't focus on anything but the fact that he could kill her before the blood in her heart would even reach her lungs.

"You're supposed to join me for dinner, Princess, or do I have to come here to escort you outside?" he asked mockingly, towering over her. "Or perhaps, it was an invitation to have dinner here," he offered, taking a sip out of the glass before placing it on the bedside table and inching closer.

Her spine straightened and she scooted in an attempt to get away from him, but ended up making a grave mistake of letting the blanket fall from her chest. Alexander's eyes darkened and he grabbed her throat before pulling her closer.

He took a seat at the edge of the bed and pulled her yet again into his lap, but this time, he didn't stop at her whimper. He used his free hand to grab the strap of her chemise and tear it apart, exposing her chest to the icy air.

"Alex," she whimpered yet again, but the sound only seemed to instigate him further, and make him dip his head in the curve of her neck.

Instead of his teeth, she felt his soft tongue o her pulse point, licking where he sucked. She couldn't stop a moan from escaping her lips that made him pull back for a brief moment to question, "Why didn't you come for dinner, my little robin?"

A hand of his found her right breast and he squeezed it, forcing another moan out of her, leaving her incapable of answering in her state. "I decided to go back to my normal sleep schedule," she managed to answer.

His lips trailed from her nape to her collarbones, sucking and kissing, as he threw another question her way, "And why is that so, if I may ask?"

"Eloise says I have lost too much weight," she blurted out the lie and felt immense pride at being able to come up with it with her head between her breasts and his lips on her sternum.

He pulled himself away and let his gaze wander over her exposed body. "Well, we must do something about that, right?" she gulped at the half-smirk and intensity behind his words. He let his hands slide over her curves for a moment before he reached out for the glass of blood on her bedside table.

"Eva!" he called out, and Eliana reached for a blanket to cover herself up but his grip made her stay still. The poor chambermaid peeked from the door leading to the dining room, but didn't dare enter. "Get me a bottle of the oldest and strongest bottle of alcohol the princess has,"

The maid scurried off and returned back in record time, yet kept her distance as she held out the bottle in his direction. He could've summouned it with his magic, but he spoke, "Come closer, Eva,"

The chambermaid gulped but complied, and Eliana felt a different form of lust at being exposed to an outsider in their moment.

"Pour it in the glass," he commanded, his voice making Eliana's lips harder. Eva nodded and obeyed without hesitation. "Good," he praised, brushing a strand of black hair behind her ears. He lowered his voice to an intimate whisper and ordered, "Now pour it on the princess,"

"W-What?" Eva asked, baffled by his request.

"You heard me. Pour it on her naked chest," he elaborated, and his crude words made her drip. Eva did as he asked her and Eliana moaned yet again-this time simply at the contact of the fluid with her bare chest. "Good girl," the Prince praised yet again, and Eliana didn't fail to noticed the lust in Eva's eyes. "Now get on your knees, Eva,"

Another gasp, but Eva obeyed again. The prince jerked Eliana's head upward before swirling the glass filled with alcohol and blood and pressing it against her lips. "Drink, princess. You look a little pale," Eliana's eyes widened, but in that moment, she would've gone as far as killing herself if that's what he asked.

"My good little robin," Eliana felt the power of his praise the same way she assumed Eva must've, and felt her body light on fire. He chugged the liquid down her throat without pulling back until she was done, and when she was, he threw the glass against the nearest wall.

The sound of the glass shattering made her jerk, and his knee pressed against her core covered by her underwear due to the movement, making her come faster than she had in the sixteen years of her existence.

She felt her juices slide down her posterior behind, and drip on his pants, in response to which, he threw her body on the bed. He pulled down his pants, uncovering his cock which was thick and hard, and looked ready to send her into the oblivion she very much craved at the moment.

Eva's lips trembled, but she understood the meaning behind his action and tentatively, took him in her mouth. Alex grabbed her wrist and placed it against his mouth before biting hard, making her moan with his cock half into her throat.

Instead of drinking it, he raised her wrist over Eliana's body and let blood drip down and over her chest covered already in alcohol. He continued for a few moments before snatching a scarf lying on the corner of her bed and tying up Eva's wrist with it.

He placed his hands on the middle of her chest where the liquid had pulled and massaged her breasts and curves as if it wasn't blood and alcohol and oil instead.

He twisted his back to face her body before lowering his head and pinching a nipple before taking another in his mouth. The coldness of the liquids was replaced by the heat of his mouth, making her moan his name. He stilled for a second during which she drove her fingers into his hair and pushed his head down, wordlessly begging him to not stop.

He took the hint and continued to suck while keeping his other hand busy with her other breast. He placed it flat against her breast before grabbing it and squeezing hard before pinching her nipple again and twisting it, making her legs jerk at the foreign feeling.

She felt another organism build up inside, as he switched to kissing her another breast and down her chest to the fabric of her underwear. He pushed her legs apart and pressed a thumb against her cotton-covered heat and rubbed it intently while capturing her breast again in his mouth.

"I think I found my favourite thing to eat: blood and alcohol off your chest. I think I would like it even better off your dripping pussy and perhaps even more if the blood is your shattered hymen,"

It all happened at once- Eva moaned, Eliana assumed because he had come in her mouth, and Alex bit on her nipple, drawing blood and quickening the pace of his rubbing until she shattered and screamed out his name, letting her upper body jerk upward.

The high lasted for a few seconds, during which Alex licked the blood trailing out of her nipple off her breast while Eva licked the cum off his dick.

She felt her eyes roll backwards once she was done and she let herself fall back on her pillow. She felt Alex rise from the bed from the way his weight disappeared and she heard Eva do the same.

In the haze, she felt someone rip off her underwear and open her legs, before a cool, wet cloth was pressed against her heat and she fell asleep to the soft wiping, and the last thing she felt was a kiss against the center of her chest and two people put a robe on her before a blanket was pulled over her body.

CHAPTER FIVE

Jason fell from his power. It crumbled and his throne was taken away from right under him, but he wasn't the only one who felt the repercussions of it. It was felt by the entire population of Ganea, and not just the pagans, but the other creatures as well.

The magic of the pagans of Ganea was bound and locked away, and another name was given to them: wiccans, a cursed species on the brink of extinction due their lost powers.

For the next three days, the kingdom had broken into chaos. All the rivers were poisoned, and the unharvested crops were infected. Ganea, once a symbol of prosperity, was reduced to a land of sickness. The King and Queen and the entire court spent those three days finding the perfect alliance.

The news of the disaster had yet to reach the other lands, hence, they concealed it cleverly and accepted one of the invitations for all three of them. Eliana's brother's engagement was broken up, and his wedding was planned with a princess belonging to a much powerful kingdom.

Roese was forced to marry the heir to the throne of the Keovalan Empire, Prince Daniel. She didn't fight the proposal, and when Eliana asked her the reason behind her sudden surrender, she told her that a princess sometimes had to sacrifice for her kingdom.

The nobles agreed that there was no time to look for a suitor for Eliana, and hence, agreed to the only proposal she had received: the one sent by the Sleyisean Empire.

Treaties were signed, and Eliana being only nine, didn't gain knowledge about all of them, but she knew the terms of the treaty concerning her like the back of her hand.

The treaty demanded gold from Ganea and in return, Sleyisea provided the country with a special kind of crop, Miocao, that was not only cheap, but also filled the stomach more efficiently than regular food.

Ganea gained water in exchange for troops of soldiers that were paid by Ganea. Peace was to be settled between the two kingdoms, and Prince Alex, and all the vampires under him were forbidden from entering the boundaries of Ganea.

The treaty was signed in blood like all the other treaties, and breaking it could prove to be catastrophic for both the parties.

Since Eliana was too young, she was only engaged to the Prince, unlike her sister, who was sent off to directly get married.

Her mother and brother had teared up at the departure of the two sisters, and Eliana had teared up as well. Her sister had remained strong, had hugged Eliana before kissing her forehead and asking her to maintain her strength.

And Eliana had needed it in her time at Sleyisea. Creatures lurked at every turn, creatures that bore no sort of mercy or kindness. The people were nice, but the beasts were too dangerous, lethal even.

But Eliana had learned. She had trained herself to be vigilant and powerful. She lacked magic, but she made up for it in the physical department. She was stronger than half the soldiers of Sleyisea. She was underweight, but that made her no less fatal, and it was all because of Alexander.

When she woke up the following morning, for a second, she wondered whether she had imagined the previous night. Thenceforth, her attention shifted to robe around her naked body, and the reality of the night was confirmed inside her mind.

She couldn't help but flush at the sinful memories. Alexander hadn't even gotten as close as to entering her, yet she had come by his mere touch. Something about the immoral act had spoken out to her, and she felt juices drip outside her solely at the memories.

Unable to help herself, she opened up her robe after casting a glance at the door leading to the other rooms into her chambers. It was open, but something about a maid walking in ignited something deeper insider her, and she tugged away her blankets as well, making herself bare to the cold winds that brushed softly against her chest, making her nipples hard.

The sun had yet not risen, and she assumed that was because she had slept through the entire day and so, she found herself seeking comfort at the fact that no would walk in and catch her doing acts that were considered filthy.

She palmed a breast of her, trying to imagine Alexander's hand instead of her own, while slipping her another hand between her thigh. She pinched her nipple, in an attempt to replicate the previous night while rubbing her fingers against her clit.

"Someone hasn't had enough," came the icy voice of the Prince. In the cloud of lust, she felt no sort of shock, but only satisfaction at his presence.

The Prince towered over her in his white tunic and brown pants looking as dark and gorgeous as night. He walked over to the open door and slammed it shut before locking it up.

His eyes scanned her naked body, trailing up and down, and he clenched his jaw at his crumbling resistance.

He grabbed a candle holder with a huge lit candle in it before making his way towards her. He used his other hand to take a pillow from the other side of the bed before placing it near her lower back, wordlessly gesturing her to lift it off the bed.

She complied and he positioned it below it before arching his back in her direction. He placed a kiss against her collarbone before gliding his jaw down towards her breasts.

Unlike her desire, she only received a singular peck over her damaged nipple, which made her groan in complaint. "Patience, my little robin,"

He hovered the candle over her chest before tilting it, letting the hot wax fall over her chest, making her yelp his name in shock as her hands fisted around the sheets.

"Sh..." he soothed her, and she watched as the wax slid down her chest before stopping in a spot below her ribs. He seemed to wait for a few seconds to let her settle before he turned over the candle again, this time right above her nipple, before doing the same with her other damaged nipple.

Eliana failed to control the moans and screams escaping her at the sudden heat, nor could she stop the wetness from making spots on her sheets. She forced her legs together as much as she could to ease some of the ache building inside her, but the Prince grabbed her knee and pushed her legs wide apart.

He lowered his head between her thighs, and just when she assumed he was going to make it better, he blew out over her aching core in a teasing manner, forcing her legs together yet again, trapping his head.

He pushed them apart and further elevated them before motioning the candleholder in the direction of her sex.

"Alex-" she started wide eyed at what he was about to do, but her silenced her with a gentle rub against her clit. He opened her legs as much as he could, exposing her pussy to the now wild winds. The cold did little to help her out, and it got even worse when pushed her folds apart and let a single drop of molten wax fall over her clit.

She immediately jolted upward at the sudden heat around her sensitive bud but his shake of head made her fall down. "Resume what you were doing before I entered," he ordered her and she grasped the solid wax on her chest and peeled it off her skin and casted it aside before palming both of her breasts with her hands.

She moaned as another drop of wax fell on her, this time over her opening, and slide inside deeper until she felt it at the very back. She pinched a nipple to distract herself from the building pressure and pleasure on the lower half of her body. Alexander continued his work, and didn't stop until she was filled with it.

He waited for it to cool down while he whisked apart her hands and seized her breasts. "Who do you imagine touching you when you come, Keizer?"

"You," she replied breathlessly, and he enveloped one of her breasts into his mouth at her response and bit it, hard enough to make another moan slip her lips but not hard enough to draw blood.

He continued ravishing her before his hands found the solid wax between her legs and he pulled it out before questioning, "If I were to make it a candle and light it on fire, would it smell like your come?"

She could only gulp in response and it seemed to please him for a smile broke across his naturally stoic face and he retreated.

"Have you had enough now or are you going to be thrusting your pretty little fingers inside when I am gone?"

"It hurts a little," she confessed, averting her gaze. Her skin was sore, and she was surprised that it wasn't bleeding out entirely. The act was good while it had lasted, but it had left a burning sort of pain in its wake.

The Prince uttered curses under his breath before taking another step away from her, and another yet again, until he was out of the door, leaving her alone and naked and feeling more exposed than she had in years.

"Higher, Your Highness," Sir Devlon guided, his voice polite. Eliana tilted the bow further upwards and aimed. She let the arrow fly out in the direction of her still target, hitting it square in her attempt.

Her practice in the dark had smoothened her archery in the daylight, leaving Sir Devlon in absolute aw. He rarely had to correct her ways or her stance, and she felt her confidence grow immensely at her skills.

The morning was rather dim for Ganea. Cloud covered the sky entirely, leaving little space for the sunlight to escape and enter the globe. The weather was chilly enough for her to wear a fluffy white jacket that eerily reminded her of her dead pet rabbit to protect herself from the harsh winds. It was a miracle that the arrow had struck the target without being wavered, but Eliana never much believed in miracles.

As suspected, she caught a mass of silver poking out from between the shrubs, and she curved her back to face Sir Devlin before questioning, "May I leave now?"

Sir Devlin gave a curt nod in response before clicking his heals and presenting her with a bow. "Your Highness,"

Eliana gave a tilt of her head in a dismissive gesture and Sir Devlin veered around and disappeared inside the castle. Eliana directed her focus back at the person cleverly concealing himself among the trees, cupped her hands around her mouth and called out, "Prince Alexander," the soldiers around her shot her a confused look, but she chose to ignore them and continued her yelling. "You can come out now!"

She saw his head move, and he stepped out of his hiding spot, and looked her straight in the eye before letting his lips curve into a wicked grin. He took perfect and practiced steps in her direction, resembling a god yet again in his movement.

"I yet again remain enchanted by your beauty, Eliana," he spoke softly, his eyes trailing from her to the sheath halter-neck dress with a keyhole and a frill at the edge that ended right below her knees.

"Again?" she asked jokingly, letting her hand glide over his sharp jawline and prominent cheekbone, before pinching his cheek in adoration. In her years with the Prince, she'd concluded that the Prince looked hot in black, handsome in white, and utterly *cute*, darling even, in royal blue.

For once, his tunic covered his chest entirely, but that didn't make him any less appealing. She felt sparks from the place where her hand rested against his face, and felt them spread all over her body till they decided to nestle in her lower belly.

"Whatever do you think you're doing?" he asked her, ignoring her question. In response, she grabbed his cheek and pressed a kiss against it, making him still.

"Don't tell me you're not okay with me kissing your cheeks when we've been far more intimate,"

"When you play with fire, *princess*, you get burned," the mocking tone in his voice at the use of the word 'princess' tore apart her good mood, and a different sort of ache developed in her chest. She let her hand fall from his cheek before turning around to leave, but she had only taken a single step before he grabbed his waist and pulled her back.

Her breath hitched from the way it affected, which was not in a good way. From a young age, she had grown a certain amount of dislike for being grabbed, and Alex knew all about it, but it seemed to have missed his mind.

Their faces were so close, the moment would've been perfect had she not begun trembling like a leaf. Alexander's eyes widened and he immediately let her out of his sinister hold on her waist.

Eliana pushed herself away from him without another thought, making hurt flash across his face. "I am sorry," she started, but her voice came out more broken than she had expected it to be.

His touch incited unwanted flashbacks, reminding her of memories she had imprisoned in a dark cage, away from her conscious, years back. On their previous two physical encounters, she was intoxicated- by the human blood and alcohol and his blood that she was certain he had added in the glass. All those elements had forced her to focus solely on the pleasure, and not on the fact that the last time she had been touched, it hadn't been consensual at all.

Alexander seemed to be able to penetrate her mind and read those dark thoughts, for he stepped back, not in a manner that suggested anyhow that he was hurt, but in a way that told her that he was giving her the space she needed.

She attempted to smile through it for his sake, but there was no way for her to suppress the reminiscences of her sexual assaults.

Instead of touching her elsewhere, the Prince put his hand on her head, and she closed her eyes at the warmth and the massaging weight. "Thanks," she whispered in a low voice, but had no clue as to what his response was, for she was far too gone in her head.

In her mind, she was in Ganea in her sister's arms, her safe place, and they were watching their brother spar with their father, and all was right.

She was brought out of her trance by coolness on her right nipple. She opened her eyes to find the Prince pressing an ice cube against her injured nipple, and her body entirely uncovered.

She was okay with touching some times, and always if there was no grabbing involved. The Prince was very well aware of her nature, and hence, his one hand was behind his back.

"I realized I never took care of you after it," the Prince spoke, making Eliana smile.

"You didn't have to. I am alright,"

He tucked a lone strand of hair behind her ear before answering. "Irrelevant," She found herself smiling at his response. He was cold yet always protective. "I had the healer make an ointment for that cut," he informed her in his usual brisk tone before retreating his hand holding the ice cube and using a cloth to wipe the wetness on her nipple.

He set the ice cube aside before taking in his hands a bowl of red paste. He took some on his fingers before gently dabbing it against her cut.

"Tell me if it hurts," he massaged the paste gently before setting it aside and wiping his hands. "How's your..." his voice trailed off as his eyes settled on her lower body.

"It hurts a tiny bit,"

"Do you want me to use an ice cube over there as well?" he asked with a devilish grin, making her eyes widen.

"No need, Your Highness," he chuckled at her expression and leaned down to press a kiss against her breastbone, sending butterflies into her stomach.

"I did not kill your maid, Eliana. Believe me if you can," the sincerity in his voice touched her heart. A part of her had always known that he would never do that, but she had witnessed women leave his chambers with blood trailing down their chest, women who were the wives of lords or even nobles.

"Then who did?" Eliana questioned, grabbing a blanket to cover her body, before rising.

"I shall find out. You have my word,"

His word.

Alexander had never once lied to her in the past seven years, and she knew that he wouldn't do it anytime soon. Her faith in him was the sole reason behind her doing everything he asked of her without raising any sort of questions.

Alexander had proven to be a dutiful main. His infidelity had nothing to do with him being an unfaithful person, but everything to do with the fact that Eliana wasn't ready to be touched by a man. In her early years, it was because she was too young, and later, it was because of her past trauma.

Alexander had been patient despite the demands raised by the royals for a child. She was his wife and he had every claim on her, yet he had not once forced her, or even tried to initiate any intimacy until two days back.

Eliana liked to tell herself that it was because she was going to Ganea and he was going to miss her, and wanted to have all of her before she left.

Alexander looked at her with adoration until they got married, and later with pure coldness, yet suddenly that had changed.

Instead of indifference, what she saw now in his eyes was much softer, and definitely a game-changer.

CHAPTER SIX

When Eliana had first arrived to Sleyisea, she had been greeted by the wolves who had tore apart the horse driving her carriage. Ganea's wealth had started depleting since the day of the curse, and hence, she had very few soldiers, who stood no chance against the pack of wolves.

A Sleyisean general who had received them, sat opposite to her in her carriage for her safety. He immediately jumped out of the carriage without a second thought and closed it safely behind himself. A howl ripped the night apart- one that despite sounding like a wolf's, belonged to a man.

Fear-laden, Eliana sat in the middle of the carriage, hugging her knees, with only her sister and Jason in her mind, as she stubbornly wished for her sister to be the last thought she had and prayed for her safety.

Body thudded against her chariot, some belonging to the soldiers, and some of the wolves, and suddenly, the noise of the violence doubled. Neighs struck across the perimeter with roars of war, and all Eliana could do was sit and pray and hope.

A few minutes later, silence enveloped the night, and the door of the carriage opened. Eliana slammed her back against the wooden confinement and backed away in fear.

The door opened revealing a young man with silver hair, yet despite that unique feature of his, the first thing to intrigue Eliana were his eyes. She noticed how the rage in them turned to hurt as he took in her trembling form.

"Please don't hurt me, Sir," Eliana sobbed, her arms caging her own self.

The hurt disappeared as soon as it had come, and he offered her a small smile which was followed by a small yet respecting bow. "Your Highness,"

He straightened his smile again before reaching out a hand in her direction. "I am Alexander, the Prince of Sleyisea,"

Yet again, when Eliana woke up, she was in her dearest husband's arms. The feeling despite being foreign, remained nothing less than amicable. Cuddling never seemed to prompt flashbacks. It somehow put her at ease and made her feel better.

With Alexander's hand on her back and their fronts pressed together, she felt nothing but safe. The man in her arms was dangerous and powerful, and had proved to be lethal to everyone but her.

She was aware that he was awake and keeping a watch on their surroundings which was comforting in its own way.

He must've sensed the fact that she had woken up, for he slide a hand across her unclothed back and curled his hand along her side. Using a single finger, he tilted her head upward and pressed a soft kiss against her forehead.

"Does it still hurt?" he asked her, retreating the finger under her chin and using the thumb of his same hand to brush against her wounded nipple. She shook her head, shocked at how she didn't feel the slightest of sting.

He retracted his other hand as well before turning her so that she laid flat on her back. He pushed a knee between hers, parting her legs, before laying a finger against her opening. Her flinch was immediate, and so was the withdrawal of his hand. She saw concern on his face for a split second before it was replaced by his smirk.

"Perhaps we shall be forced to use the ice cubes now,"

She slapped a palm against his chest playfully before jabbing a finger against it. "You want me to believe that if you start pushing ice in my vagina, you won't be tempted to push in something else?"

He gasped dramatically. "I am a man of control, Eliana. However can you doubt my control when I have been controlling myself for the past seven years?"

"Well, if you hadn't been, then you would've been a certified paedophile,"

Another gasp. "Be grateful, Keizer,"

"I am," she spoke, switching her tone immediately from joking to soft.

"And I shall stay in control for however long you want,"

"I am grateful for that as well," she uttered, staring deep into his grey eyes. They were indeed hypnotising, sending her into a different and new sort of oblivion, making her feel lost.

Out of nowhere, Alexander grabbed her head and pressed his lips against hers for the first time in seven years. She grasped his head and kissed him back with the same need and passion, pulling him closer to herself.

The kiss was beautiful enough to remove all oxygen from her lungs and replace her blood with unadulterated drugs, providing her a novel high. He devoured her lips mercilessly yet gently at the same time. Her worked on her lower lips before pulling back a little to capture her upper lip, lazily flicking his tongue against her lip.

Uncertain as to what to do, she started sucking on his lower lip, but that seemed to unsatisfy him, for her took a hold of one of her breasts and cradled it in his palm before pinching her nipple, making her gasp.

He took it as an opportunity to let his tongue wander in her mouth, swiping and licking at every corner. When he pulled back, she was flustered and soaking wet. The kiss was magical and demanding enough to turn Alexander's eyes to black.

Suddenly, the sweet Alex vanished, leaving in his stead a roaring beast, who curled his body forward before biting down hard on her neck. This time, it wasn't a nip. She felt him extend his fangs inside her.

She screamed- from pleasure or pain she knew not, but her hands remained on his back, pressing her towards herself, in an attempt to not let him get away.

The light-headedness came instantly for the blood loss and weight loss didn't bode well. He must've sensed it and she could only assume that it was the reason why he pulled back. He reached into his pocket to retrieve two pearls with pointed extensions.

Eliana's eyes widened with fear and horror as he sunk them into the holes in her neck. The blood pins were made for slaves of the vampires. Vampires kept the blood pins plugged into their necks or wrists, and whenever the felt hungry, they simply removed the blood pins and drank their blood without having to go through the trouble of tearing through their skin.

They were created not only for the sole benefit of the vampires but the slaves as well. The vampires preferred to drink the blood of the slaves every day which forced them to rip through half-healed skin. By using the blood pins they halted the healing of the skin altogether, and the blood pins even stopped any sort of infection.

Alexander leaned once again to lick the residual blood on the sides of the blood pins before pulling back for good. He pushed her breasts up before planting a kiss in the centre of her chest- her favourite place, making her blush irrepressibly. The kiss was tender and she noticed that whatever beast had awoken inside him had gone back to sleep for his eyes were grey again.

"How am I ever going to live with you gone?" he asked, more to himself than to her, before selectively crashing his weight on her and resting his head on her chest. His words pulled her heart in a chokehold, and for a second, she wished to stay in Sleyisea forever, especially in his arms but she pushed those thoughts aside. It had been years since she'd seen her parents, and she desperately wanted to meet them again.

"It's only a matter of a few days," she consoled him, running her fingers soothingly through his silver locks. He shifted his weight on the other hand before caressing the side of her breast with other. The touch wasn't lustful in the least, instead it was hungry in a different sort of way.

Eliana had no idea as to why his behaviour had shifted so suddenly in the past few days, but she was grateful for it. From a caring...stranger, he had morphed into a loving husband, and Eliana assumed it was because of the fact that she was leaving for Ganea.

Only then did it cross her mind that Alex was afraid. He was afraid that she was going to leave and never return.

"You're so warm," he muttered pressing idle pecks over her chest and tugging her breasts closer to him.

"I will come back. You know that, right?" she felt his nod against her chest and she gently massaged his scalp. "Is that why you have been behaving differently? Are you anxious that I won't return?"

In response, he intensified his hold on her and let a languid moment pass before raising his head and looking at her in the eye. "I'll hunt you down if I have to, Eliana," All those words but none denying his fear.

"Then why the change, Alex?"

"I realized that you were old enough and I no longer had to restrain myself in the fear of traumatising or hurting you," he simply responded before tugging her upwards and rolling over to the side so she was by his side. She undid the knot on his tunic before letting him pull her into his arms.

He rubbed his hands on her back and she locked hers behind his neck. The moment wasn't sexual, it was rather comforting. Eliana wasn't aware as to how much she needed it until she had felt it. All those preparations for Ganea had pushed the fact that she would be staying without him to the back of her mind.

Sleyisea had been her home for the past seven years, *the Prince* had been her home for the last seven years. Without a warning, emotions started surging through her chest. The day was almost a fortnight away and she experienced the urge to savour every moment with him and Sleyisea.

"We'll be fine..." the Prince murmured in her ears, tightening his grip around her before to stroking her head till sleep pulled her into oblivion.

Once again, she woke up naked with a thing blanket draped over her. Light seeped through the gap between the curtains, shining directly over her body. "Has anyone ever told you how gorgeous you look when you're naked and the sun is illuminating you as if you were a goddess?" came a husky voice from the other end of the room.

There stood the Prince leaning against the door while wearing nothing but a pair of pants and a bracelet that matched the one on her wrist.

Pressing a hand against her blanket to keep it from falling over, Eliana slowly got to her feet before answering, "No, you're the first,"

"Good," the Prince hummed, and his approval yet again sparked something in her chest. He offered her a hand and she slipped hers in it, interwinning their fingers. "You can let go of the blanket, Princess, it's nothing I haven't seen before,"

Her face flushed and she responded, "I am starving. I need food, Alex,"

"Well, I don't know about you, but I would rather have you for breakfast," he whispered, ripping the blanket away and bending his body to engulf her breasts in his mouth, "And lunch," he added, nipping on her nipple. "And dinner," he gave her breast a small mock-bite before pulling away. "You sure your hunger cannot wait?"

Despite the heat coiling in her lower belly, she shook her head, making him sigh jestingly. He picked up a chemise belonging to her that lay on a chair and pulled it down her body. Eliana was grateful for coverage despite how little the dress actually enclosed, thhe foremost reason for her gratitude being the dress obscuring her naked self from the eyes of the Prince, and the second reason being the shielding the dress provided her from the turbulent winds.

The Prince pulled back a seat for her, wordlessly gesturing her to sit. In front of her lay platters amassed from kingdoms many. Eliana could recall eating them-some in feasts hosted by the rulers of the strongest of empires to have ever existed, and some at her own wedding.

Never had she witness all of them occurring collectively and simply being set on her table as if it was normal for them all to be present in the room of a mere princess.

"How did you manage to pull all of this together?" she gasped, her hand flying to cover her open mouth.

"The 'how' isn't substantial in the least, princess," he replied, a hint of caring coating his tone. He emptied spoonful of varieties onto her plate, and when she declared she couldn't take another bite, he took it into his own hand and fed her until he deemed enough.

Post that, he declared that he had some tasks to look after and would be gone a long while, presumably, till the nightfall. Despite her clenching heart, Eliana made no move to restrain him, afraid of being a barrier between him and his work. He was a prince and he had duties towards his kingdom.

That afternoon, Eliana had to attend a small party hosted by the Queen Auriol in the honor of her pregnancy. The King had demanded a feast, the Queen wanted something private as she believed that being out in open with so many people could end up with one of them cursing her and her unborn child.

The Queen had been right, for the talisman that protected her from black magic had been used to its full capacity in the first three days of the announcement in spite of never leaving the confinements of the castle.

Auriol was not much older than Eliana herself: only twenty, but she was more fit to rule Sleyisea than Eliana could ever be. Eliana had found herself protected from the horrors of the land by the Prince. Sleyisea was known for its monsters: wolves, witches, vampires, kishis, pagans, heretics, nymphs, dryads, kelpies, sirens, fae and whatnots, all divided into different territories at all times except when they fought in wars.

Sleyisean wars were often the most beautifully hauntings things one could ever witness. Different kinds of warriors moved together as a unit, setting their personal grievances aside and behaving as immortals, tearing through ranks of soldiers.

Sleyisea had never once been taken over by another empire cause of it's strength. The subjects fought amongst each other, but when push came to shove, they had each others' backs and there, the birth of the babe in Auriol's womb was to mark the onset the fiftieth generation of its dynasty, the pride of which was evident on King Thaddeus's face as he addressed all the guests.

"I welcome you all to this small lunch hosted by my wife. May your blessing be with her and the heir of Sleyisea,"

The King was a man of a few words, Eliana rarely heard him speak, even during the brunches they often had together as a family, so she wasn't surprised by the lack of words.

What did shock her was the way his arm was wrung around Auriol's waist, holding her as if she were the tenderest and the most valuable thing. Perhaps there was some sort of redemption for the King after all, something that would pull him out of his closed-off bubble. One could only hope.

Eliana possessed no genuine friends. All her ladies in waiting from Ganea had been married off to Lords living in faraway lands and the wives of the ones resided in the lands were solely poisonous.

She could see Celeste, the wife of Sir Maggart, a honourable knight of age eighty, sweettalking to the King in hopes of becoming his mistress and gaining a position when her husband were to die.

The move reeked of desperateness-pulling things so depraved at such an occasion only proved how careless and power-hungry she was. A circle of ladies pointed at Celeste and gossiped, but Eliana knew better than to join them. They had proved to strike just as low, and she knew for a fact that three of them had been in bed with her husband.

One of them, Lady Aurora, seemed to notice her staring and Eliana quickly looked away. She picked a corner spot and made herself comfortable, quietly staring out the window while waiting for the food.

"Well, hello, *princess*," came a mocking sound from Lady Twila, an active member of the secret husband-stealer club. She wore a gorgeous gown with a sweetheart neckline with two slits beneath her breasts, putting their folds on display. It was evident that she was there for the same purpose as Celeste, she had only chosen to be more discrete about her target.

But the sultriness of the dress hadn't cut her, it was it's color. Twila, was wearing red, *her* color. Eliana pushed away the rage and barred herself for the comments she was about to receive.

"How's Alexander?" she asked Eliana, a smirk playing on her lips. She had slept with him, Eliana knew that for they'd "accidently" bumped into each other when she was leaving his chambers and Eliana was leaving hers.

"He's fine," Eliana replied dryly, in no mood to engage in a passive fight.

"Just fine? Last I saw him, he was much more than fine," the insinuation behind her words making the ladies surrounding her laugh. Eliana bit back a reply and turned her focus back to the sceanery. Twila threw a scrutnising glare over her body before continuing, "Or perhaps it's for he is confided in your tedious company. After all, you are a young girl with little experience, you mustn't be able to keep him satisfied,"

"I have heard that Alex didn't prefer skinny girls," another lady, Lady Este, added, and all of them burst simultaneously in a fit of practiced laughter.

"I don't recall giving you the permission to address me by anything but 'Your Highness'," a cold voice tore through the laughter, making them all freeze.

You will watch your tongue when you speak to my wife," Alex added, wrapping an arm around Eliana's waist and pulling her in an embrace. He kissed her forehead tenderly before turning back to the ladies. "Or I'll cut your tongue off,"

"Your Highness, I-" Twila began, but Alexander interrupted her.

"Or maybe, I'll keep it so you could use it to confess your sins to your husbands, who'll have you hanged for adultery, and I won't stop him," Eliana found his voice lowered to a deathly whisper. "I'll have you know, my wife's body is meant for my divine worship, unlike your whore's body which is only meant for fucking," with those words, he pulled Eliana closer, tucking her head under his chine before turning to Este. "And as for my preferences, Lady Este, I prefer women who don't undress for money and jewels and then claim to be chaste and pure. I like prostitutes who accept their identity and virgins who are who they claim to be," His eyes darkened as he took another step in her direction and threatened, "Next time, you shall address her as 'Princess Eliana' or 'Your Highness'. I could claim your disrespect to a royal as treason and have you beheaded, or thrown to the mercy of the wolves,"

Twila's face fell from the daunting puzzle it resembled when she'd tried to cut Alexander off to take after the expression of a mouse caught in a trap. She fumbled for words, and Alexander silkily offered,

"I suppose the words you're looking for run along the lines of 'I am sorry' consisting of different forms of apologies, varying from but not limited to kissing her shoes and falling to your knees,"

Twila's small painted face became red-whether with fury or discomfiture, Eliana knew not. She stared at the Prince with disbelief, waiting for him to let her out of his field of vision and to leave her be, but the Prince's gaze remained unwavering. He seemed to conclude that she needed more motivation, for he extended his fangs and snarled, "Kneel,"

Eliana's eyes widened with horror and she turned to look at him to silently plea him to withdraw himself from the drama he was planning, however, the expression on his face scared even her.

Twila's whole body vibrated with fear and humiliation as she sank to her knees and bowed her head. Alex's face twisted into a smirk as he got down on a knee as well beside Twila.

Eliana didn't bother hiding the shock on her face, not when simultaneously all the ladies let out a gasp. His fingers curled around the hem of her skirt and he hitched it up to expose her ankles and her heels.

He traced a knuckle from a vein on the side of her ankle to the front of her heels before smearing his fingers against a spec of dust that had collected on her heels. "They look rather sullied, don't you agree, Twila?" he purred. "Why don't you do the Prince a favour and lick them clean?"

A tears fell on her feet making Eliana intervene, "I don't want her filthy mouth near even my shoes," she declared, before bending over and grabbing the Prince by his hair before crashing her lips down on his.

The Prince aided her giving them the spectacle Eliana desired. "Aren't you the most gorgeous woman to have walked the planet?" Eliana smiled coyly against his lips before pulling him to his feet.

The ladies surrounding them had entered a phase of shock and rage as they gaped at the scene unfolding before them. Hundreds of years, and the Prince had never claimed a lady like that, had never went down on his knees and brushed her heels, had never treated a woman the way he had treated her.

His kindness known to be rare, his care practically inexistent, and his love, dead. Such gentleness was sure going to incite gossip, and for once, Eliana found herself rooting for it.

Alexander curled an arm around her waist, his touch sending delicious chills even with all the clothes that covered her body, and they sauntered to the outside of the room together.

"I need food, Alexander, we need to go back inside," Eliana hissed once they were far from the others' earshot.

"I need my wife, Eliana," his words remained flirtacious while his lips curled into a smile savage enough to make Eliana gulp as his eyes flashed with pure lividness. His fingers found her throat and he squeezed, sending jitters of pain from the blood pin down her chest. "Next time someone disrespects you, my darling wife, you fight back," he released his grip on her waist to roughly grab a hold of her face. "You are a princess, Eliana. Learn to act like one," his grip tightened, both around her neck and her face, making tears pool in her eyes, not from pain, but rather from the memories.

She hated being grabbed roughly, and no one remained the exception to that, even the Prince, and he was aware of it.

Suddenly, the Prince's face was replaced by the face of another man- older, with grey hair and a long beard and a scar running from his eyebrows to his chin, but he wsn't a warrior.

Fear sluiced through her veins and settled around her heart as she fought to blink away those images, but Alex didn't make it easy for her.

Her vision blurred furthermore as a lone tears carved it's path down her dry cheeks. She felt the hands retreat, but her mind was too far gone to see it for herself.

"Eliana," she heard his despaired voice, but stepped away from his presence. She picked up her skirt, turned on her heels and fled the hallway, screams restounding inside her head.

She ran and ran until she came across her room, and without sparing back a glance, she pushed open the door and kicked out her staff. When the last guard was gone, she locked the door behind him and moved over her dresses to cover it, in case someone decided to tear it open.

When she was satisfied with the counterfeit security she had crafted around herself, she let herself sink to the floor and wept.

CHAPTER SEVEN

Alexander allowed her the space she needed, for it had slipped his mind for a moment that she was a mere wiccan and a person with a haunting past. He had touched her when she had required some distance to breath, had grabbed her when she had seen a protector in him.

His rage, that was purely directed towards the mindless ladies, had instead hunted down Eliana's soul and had tried to burn it with its wild embers, had tried to turn all she was to ash.

Deep down, Alexander was well aware, that if he hadn't noticed the tears when he had, if he hadn't regained the control when he had, he would've killed it. He would've feasted on her until the blood in the deepest of the arteries had run dry and she would've fell to the floor in pieces. Her head, her wrists, her ankles, they would all have been lying apart, assembling nothing less horrifying than a ritual made to please the devil himself.

Then again, he was the devil. His wings had been chopped off and he was cursed for eternity to do nothing but drain the lives of innocents, hypothetically, for in real life, he had been the one to make that choice. He had chosen to be the violent immortal being the gods had cursed him to be, in return having more time to find his sister, Avaluna.

While his curse was bloodthirst, Avaluna's remained unparalleled power; raw and inexhaustible, strong enough to give her the strength to be able to challenge a god. She was a goddess in being, blessed by seventeen deities to bear exceptional looks, irresistible charm, and magical powers that could crumble empires.

Their mother, Eiusi, was the goddess of virtues. A sworn celibate, she had birthed them both using forbidden magic, that had put a target on her back. They had been hunted their whole lives, until he was six and Avaluna, two. They had been caught, and while their mother's lifeforce was drained, they had used that power to make the two of them immortals, until Lobium had declared that Avaluna's role was to be played later and he had taken her away.

Alexander's curse kicked in when he turned twenty-one, and he scoured the ends of the earth in search of his sister, but found no trace. He could not enter heaven because of the devil he had been made into, yet he never failed to attempt all the possible ways, even as the stairs burned him, the doorknob pierced through his hand and darkness tried and tried to consume him whole, and when he realized he couldn't get to heaven, he began assembling forces to prepare for a war against the gods.

His efforts were all in vain as no fleet of ships, or unit of soldiers could as much as get past the threshold, much less attack. The gates of heaven were forged with iron and silver and gold and ever element that could ward off beasts.

He had spent centuries looking for his sister, and then, for a purpose, but found none, until he heard of the birth of the second princess of Ganea, Eliana Keizer, and he suddenly knew who he was going to live for again, yet somewhere down the road, so many mistakes had been made, fate, that had brought them together, had tore them apart time and time again, this time in form of wrath.

There was nothing worse than a vampire's ire, especially when their mate was concerned, and he had mistakenly let his fury loose in front of her, knowing damn well that she hated aggressive grabs, hated how they reminded her of another time when he had failed to protect her.

When Eliana had only just arrived in Sleyisea, the Queen of that time, Estelle, had made sure that she felt comfortable in the kingdom. She was one of the few royals of Sleyisea who withheld some sort of compassion, and when Alexander had confessed to her that Eliana was his mate, she had taken it upon herself to treat her the way she deserved.

Estelle had her own designers create a gown fit for a goddess, quite literally so. Eliana had arrived with her own engagement gown made by the designers of Ganea, but it didn't hold a candle to the one Estelle had created.

She adorned her with jewelleries crafted from gems that were extracted from fallen stars and metiorites. Every piece of the outfit was worth more diamonds than the ones they'd taken from Ganea from the treaty, and it was only fair.

He had slipped a ring fit for her tiny hand in front of a crowd and had sank to his knees for that. He had stayed that way for her to slip the ring through his fingers and had pressed a hand against her trembling head to sooth her. She was Sleyisea's property then, and was no doubt afraid that he was going to hurt her, *touch* her, yet Alexander felt no sort of lust towards her. She was a child. He only felt protectiveness and care, only felt the need to hold her to comfort her and promise her that he'll scare away all the demons that would come after her.

A foolish server had handed her a glass of champagne and Eliana had almost sipped it, innocent to its contents. Fortunately, Alexander had found out about it, and had gotten the server out on the spot for his foolishness.

Later that night, he had drawn her away from the celebrations, desperate to hold her shaking frame as she contemplated what he would do to her, yet thought better and let his actions show his sincerity.

He reached into his bracelet and pulled out a bracelet he had forged for her. It bore no visible magic, and its only purpose was to provide the wearer strength, both physical and mental.

The bracelet had another spell on it, one that called out to him whenever she was in any sort of danger, for she had a replica of it on his wrist.

He carefully took her hand in his and wrapped the bracelet around her small wrist. Her curious eyes lingered on the silver carvings of the bracelet and the red stones along the length of it before she turned her gaze to look him in the eyes.

"You have pretty eyes," she had spoken, her first casual sentence to him since he'd rescued her from the wolves, since they'd met for the first time. Those words did something to the cold heart he had possessed for centuries, and the candour in her eyes touched him.

She had told him his eyes were pretty, and had meant it, had believed it. Most people were unnerved by the grey coldness sucking their souls deep inside with a single look, yet that nine year old girl found them 'pretty'. Not scary, not haunting, 'pretty', and he knew he was going to keep her forever.

Her eyes dropped to the black bracelet around his own wrist and she smiled- the most beautiful sight he had ever witnessed, before slowly nudging his bracelet with hers to make peaceful clinking sounds. She giggled to herself for a minute before looking at me back in the eyes and saying, "Thank you,"

He didn't ask her to not thank him for he was her fiancé and was doing his job. She wasn't a job, saving her was need, necessity and he didn't want her to feel otherwise.

He patted her head, ran a hand through her hair before pulling her back inside the castle and taking her to her chambers. She had been living them since she arrived to the days leading up to their engagement, and nothing was different, except she was his and not only on paper.

The ring on her finger- the diamond with eight drops of his own blood, proved that. He could've chosen a red diamond to begin with, but something about ruining the crystal clear diamond and tainting it with his blood spoke to him, for he could see her as a pure diamond, and he wanted to be her sole damnation, the darkness blanketing her fire, not quenching it, yet turning it into something that could make eyes bleed by a mere glance, for light could never solely exist. Light was always generated from twisting and turning flames, restlessness burning to be. He wanted to be the fluid darkness that would put the flames at an unnatural ease and morph them into something that was just as viscious, but it remained at peace at it's core.

Diamonds were known for their clarity, their color, and if possible, she was one of the clearest of the diamond, with no tint, as if made for him to add a hue in the way he pleased, and Eliana was more than happy to let him do that.

That day forth, Eliana always wore red. At first, he assumed it was to match the jewelery he had gotten her, yet later, he realized, it was to indicate that she was accepting her fate. She was a vampire's wife, the princess consort of

Sleyisea, and she was embracing the dark reality that came with it.

The submissiveness in her reached out to his darkness, and he didn't once mistake it for weakness. Eliana would listen if she wasn't in power, but that never meant that she would tolerate everything, just as she shouldn't.

She was raised to be an obedient wife, but Roese had added something in her personality that made her fierce, and if he were a fool, he would've never been able to sense the magic coursing through her blood, thrashing at her skin.

Yet, she never fought back apart from being sarcastic whenever he teased her, and even that remained rare. She never argued with anyone, did what she was asked to, and kept her head low like she was a maid.

He had tolerated it for seven years, had allowed to grow into a confident young woman who could stand up for herself, yet she hadn't. She smothered her powers, and became a porcelain doll, ready to do anything anyone asked of her.

He couldn't take it when she was taunted by women she had more power than, women who were in all ways inferior, and he had let his anger take the reins, and it had ended up horrifically.

He gave her a few hours of space, in case she couldn't hold it together if she was approached by him again so quickly, yet when he reached her chambers, he was greeted with silence.

There was eerie quiet bubbling inside, unusual for a chamber filled with chambermaids hustling around. "What is going on?" He questioned the guards stationed outside her room.

"The princess requested all the chambermaids and guards to leave and has been inside ever since," the guard answered, keeping his gaze away.

Alexander pushed away the darkness offering him what could be inside, and simply knocked on the door with all the restraint he had.

No reply came, and he barely stopped himself from breaking the door, which he couldn't, anyways, since it was forged to keep away the demons. No one could break it open, no amount of power would be enough to tear it apart, and he was well aware of that, but if it came to that, he would try.

"El, darling, open up!" he ordered, keeping his voice as soft as he could, so as to not give her another scare. She didn't adhere to his command and whether his voice reached her, he knew not, he could only hope. "Eliana!" he yelled this time, praying to the gods he often cursed that the voice would reach her.

Yet again, there was no response. No sound greeted him, no shift fell upon his immortal and hyperexcitable ears. Unable to keep his rage reeled in, he slammed his fist against the door, and the door visibly shook and some shards of wood cute his skin open.

In response, he hears a small gasp, a sound that lasts for the smallest of the moments as if it had slipped her and she wanted to swallow it back. As if she believed that the beasts would catch her if she let slightest of a sound escape her.

She was wrong.

The beasts would catch her anyways.

He took a step back before slamming his entire body against the door, yet it only gave a single rattle. He retreated it, and repeated his moves, again, and again, and again, and was about to go at it another time when he felt raw magic push him away.

The door crashed open, intriguingly, not from the outside but the inside, and it wasn't from physical force.

Around him, soldier crumbled to the floor like sacs of miocao, and the power even slammed him against the wall facing the door. His eyes trailed to the dead guards lying on the foot of the door, and he instantly ran to the room.

"Eliana!" he shouted, rushing past the door with an inhuman speed. At first glance, the room appeared unoccupied; the bed was made, the curtains pushed open, the door leading to the other rooms was wide open, and there was no one in sight. Not a soul.

But he could hear the thundering heartbeats, the ravaged breathes, the tremors, and he approached the small corner beside the bed. He made his footsteps soft yet audible- not in a haunting clicking way, but in a way that told her that he was approaching her, so he wouldn't take her by surprise.

He finds her trembling form on the floor with legs folded and tucked inside her arms, hugging her knees in a protective stance with tears streaming down her face. The sight crushed the demon part of his, his immortal soul who had claimed her as his mate, and he knelt down to match her height.

She looked up at him behind from behind the tears and a sob wrecked through her body. "I am right here, my little robin, and I am not going to let anyone hurt you," he reached out a hand but slowed down his movements as it almost fell against her face until he was certain she wouldn't resist his touch.

He cupped her cheeks and her face moulded into his palm, his fingers long enough to engulf half of it. He let his other hand tenderly grabbed a hold of hers and he unlocked the grip she had around herself and let her legs relax.

More tears spilled from her eyes making his jaw clench. "Whatever I have to do, I'll get it done, my dead robin, but please, for my sake, stop crying," he pleaded, wiping the flowing tears.

Another sob before she replied, "Please don't grab me," he withdrew his hands at the speed of light, yet his gaze devoured her, scoured inside her mind and raged over her body to find any other cause of her discomfort.

"I am so very sorry, Eliana, please forgive me,"

In response, he violently shook her head before uttering, "Please don't apologise, you're not the one at fault, Your Highness. I simply can't seem to get images out of my mind,"

Images of the time he'd failed her yet again as her mate, and even as her fiancé. He forced the guilt of his mind before focusing on another important matter.

"The force of power I felt, did that come from within you, Eliana?" he questioned, his eyes trailing around the room to find any other presence, only to return back empty-handed to Eliana.

"I am not sure. I heard your voice, Alexander, I heard you calling out my name, but I was so afraid that it was going to be someone else, I assumed it was my mind plying tricks on me, and if I were to open the door, he would enter and...he would destroy me. When the thrashing began, I only became more frightened, and something happened. I believe I screamed ferousciously yet silently, and it turned out to be loud enough to shatter it all,"

"Eliana," he started, as gently as you could. "I am not certain as to what form of magic you used, but that door..." he let his eyes travel to the broken pieces of the door. "It's impervious to magic and brute strength. Apart from the lock placed within, only the gods could've opened it. I am five hundred years old, Eliana, and even my power only managed to rattle it,"

The tears started disappearing from her eyes as the sincerity of the matter dawned upon her. Alexander withheld the information about the dead guards from her to keep the guilt at bay, guilt that was ravish her and leave her crumbled if she were to find out that she was responsible for the death of the men who'd risked their lives time and time again to protect her.

She pressed her palms flat against the material of her dress and smoothened it before exhaling and tucking a strand of hair behind her ear.

It was only then did I noticed that a lock of her black hair had turned white, and not only from the roots, and I had the feeling, that the reason behind the transition had nothing to do with aging, but everything to do with the powers she had displayed.

CHAPTER EIGHT

Her first few days in Sleyisea, Eliana was taken on tours around the castle on royal grounds by the knights. Estelle, the then Queen of Sleyisea had often accompanied her on her expenditures.

She had the kindest soul Eliana had ever come across. Her smile was known to set the darkest streets of Sleyisea alight, including the depraved soul of the king. Estelle, unlike Eliana had married out of love, and that had altered the history of Sleyisea. A land, once known for the beasts crawling over it, had found some sort of light in the form of a queen, and Eliana had as well.

One day, they were in a remote wing of a mansion near the castle belonging to a Lord who hosted a feast in her honor. Eliana was quietly getting ready in a guestroom, alone apart from two maids who were helping her get dressed, when the door of her room had been violently opened.

She was expecting no one but the Queen, and so, she ignored the feeling crawling up, whispering down slowly that something wasn't fine. Heavy, aggressive footsteps approached her, making her turn around sharply.

In a matter of seconds, the two maids were heaps of bodies on the floor, and a firm hand had been pushed against her mouth, keeping any voice from escaping. Brutal blue eyes came into the view, eyes belonging to a man with bright white hair and face adorned with scars. His eyes were devoid of any emotions, and stared up at her as if she were a mere object that he was to wield to fulfil his promises.

Two men were at his sides. One of them was bulkier while the other was taller. The white-haired men gave a small yet unmissable signal, and the two men grabbed Eliana's fragile, flailing arms. The white-haired man's hand was replaced by the bulky man, covering up a portion of her nose as well, inhibiting entry of air.

The white-haired man's hand came down on her camisole-the only piece of clothing covering her body and her gripping it's front and pulled it, tearing the thin piece of clothing, leaving her bare. His hands came on her thighs, and only one thought rang in her mind,

Alex, Alex, Alex.

She merely had to touch her bracelet, yet it was difficult with the iron grip of the two men. She chanelled all her strength in a single tug and managed to curl out her fingers from the hold of the tall men and used them to touch the cool metal dangling against the wrist of the same hand.

A part of her screamed that perhaps the gift was only sentimental and that perhaps it bore no magic, and wouldn't summoun Alex, yet somehow, she chose to believe.

She chose to believe as rough hands grabbed her, touched her everywhere prior to pulling apart her legs before leaving her altogether to pull down the pants of the white-haired man. One second, the men around her had their eyes glinting with malice, the next, there was nothing in their eyes, and their bodies were heaps on the floor, lying beside the lifeless maids.

The Prince stood in front of her, his chest rising and falling in an uneven rhythm, her eyes depicting nothing but rage as they moved all over the scene. Realization dawned upon him in a fraction of a moment and he took off his jacket and offered it to her, his gaze casted on the floor.

She slowly wrapped it around herself before folding her arms around herself before a sob escaped her lips. She let herself fall to the floor as one after other tears drove past her lashes and dripped against the marble. If her mother were to see her, she would scold her and call it out of etiquette for a woman of her standing, but Eliana couldn't find it in herself to care.

Alexander got to his knees beside her, and his first reaction appeared to be to reach out to her and hold her cheeks, yet he seemed to think otherwise when Eliana flinched away from his touch. He pressed his eyes close and in a few seconds, Estelle appeared in the room, running towards where Eliana laid on the floor.

Alexander backed away and left, but Eliana didn't miss the remorse on his face. She wanted nothing more than to scream at him and tell him that he wasn't at fault, and he was her saviour, yet words betrayed her.

Yet, when he found her crumbled on the floor seven years later, she chose to voice her thoughts instead of letting the guilt suffocate him.

"It was not your fault," five words that seemed to shatter his icy composure and leak raw emotions through the cracks. Eyes boring into hers, he ran a finger through the side of his face before letting them tangle inside her hair. Softly, he tugged her head backwards before curling a lone strand around his finger.

"Eliana," he voice her name in a way one would hum a melody, and she rubbed her thumb against his lips before a broken voice escaped her,

"I don't know what happened to me, Alex," the honesty appeared to hit him square in the chest for the grey of his eyes broke for a fraction of a second before putting itself back together. He seemed to contemplate his response for a moment, for when he answered, his gaze was feather-like, brushing against the skin it touched.

"A lock of your hair has turned white, Eliana,"

A gasp broke free from her lips and instantly tugged the strand way from his hold to take a look. The pure white strand was no short of enticing in its own way, it's texture similar to that of a newborn rose.

"This can't be happening! I am not old!"

"This has nothing to do with become old, my little robin. I believe it is caused by those miraculous powers you just displayed. It looks like some sort of a transformation to me,"

"The magic escaped my system long back, Alex, however could I have done that? Could it be a curse?" she question, despite knowing the answer. The bracelet on her hand kept all the curses at bay despite the one coursing through her blood.

As expected, Alexander gave a shake of a head before pulling her to her feet. "I shall ask around, El, we'll find something," the certainty in his voice would've fooled her had she not known him well enough.

He patted the sides of her dress before placing a chaste kiss against her forehead. On normal occasions, the kiss would've sent her heart into a blissful oblivion, yet the circumstances made her ignore it wholeheartedly. No sliver of comfort crept down her spine, no shiver made her skin crawl, if there was any heat in the kiss, it was absorbed by the coldness that seemed to be leaking from her body.

He noticed the indifference in her body language and guided her to the dinning table of her room. In a matter of minutes, the maids had served food on the table and Eliana was done with it by the end of a minute.

After devouring the contents of the food given to her by Alex, Eliana rose and allowed herself to rest. Alexander, for once, stayed by her side at least until the caress of the winds finally pulled her to sleep.

Ravens pounding their beaks against the window broke her peaceful slumber, forcing her to her feet. Five ravens raked their black eyes over her, their gaze penetrating to her soul. Her fingers curled around the pillow to her side and she threw it at the closed window in hopes to scare away the wild birds.

The pillow collided with the window with a thud and slid down the glass with a toe-curling sound, and the birds instantly fled. "Poor birds," Alexander spoke, clicking his tongue playfully. Eliana jumped at the sound of his voice, not expecting his presence to last till the morning.

"You're killing my heart, Your Highness," she gasped, one hand clutching her chest while the other working on patting down her hair.

"No different from what you're doing to mine," he took her hand in his and placed it against his heart. Seven years of loving the Prince from afar had finally led to this, the warmth and loved Eliana had craved since the beginning, yet something deep in her stomach warned her to not get too comfortable.

Moods were fleeting, people were fleeting, and in Eliana's life, even her magic had failed to prove to be a constant, whatever would a mere vampire prove to be? Yet, she thrived in the moment, revelling in the power she held over the Prince and his wraith heart.

Her lips curved into a smile of their own accordance, and Eliana cupped his cheek to pull his face closer to hers before pressing a kiss against the other one. "Thank you so much for everything you've done for me, Alexander,"

In response, he claimed her lips in a passionate yet short-lived kiss that failed to erase the dreadful memories of the previous night. "I have reached out to a hermit," he spoke, as if they shared the same thoughts. "I sent an acolyte to gain more knowledge on the subject. Until then, we shall have to keep it from prying eyes.

"I understand,"

A finger of his reached out to pull apart the white strand from the rest of her hair and he tugged on it before letting it break free and curl backwards. "You must take care of it. I'll have some dye sent over for you if you wish to use it, though I hardly believe there are other alternatives,"

She offered an absent-minded nod in response before sitting back down on the bed. "Do you believe it has something to do with the cursed placed upon Ganea and Jason?" she asked quietly. The curse had stolen her magic seven years back, and it seemed to be the only thing capable of returning it.

"Even if the curse on you were to be removed, you could never produce magic so potent to tear through a door capable of keeping half the gods at bay. So much magic in the body of a mortal is unfeasible. Unbearable, even. Unless, you are an offspring of a god or a goddess..." he added quietly, the unsaid question evident in his eyes.

Eliana shook her head at the mere thought of her mother engaging in adultery. "My father had it confirmed, time and time again, that I only bore pagan blood and his blood. He was never the trusting type, despite how much love my mother carried for him in her heart. I believe it is still the same."

The silence in the room was lethal enough to make Eliana throw a pointless question his way, if only to pierce it. "Could a curse be that powerful?"

"Only if it were bestowed by a being equally powerful,"

She nodded before patting the space to her right, wordlessly asking him to sit down. He did so without hesitation and wrapped an arm around her should before drawing her closer to himself.

"I never got the chance to apologize," he whispered, pressing a peck against her temple. "Forgive me what I did in the hallway yesterday, Eliana. You became the outlet of my rage, wrongly so. The fault was mine, and while I understand that no excuse could ever justify my actions, I just wish for you to know that I cannot stand anyone disrespecting you. It tears me apart when anyone merely graces you with an insulting glance,"

"I understand why you did it, Alex, and while I would love to lie and say that it didn't hurt me, I cannot do that. But I forgive you in hopes that you will hold that temper in the future,"

"I will. And next time anyone degrades you, do not hesitate in showing them the princess you are,"

"I shall not," she whispered back a promise.

Morning came and bled away while she waited for any appearance that could be made by the Prince but none came.

She was exhausted by the time the day had ended, yet didn't back away from their daily rituals. Three days, they had only three days left until she were to board the carriage that were to take her away to her homeland, and sudden dread was starting to sneak up on her.

She was certain it was just the nerves, nothing related to her gut, yet a whispered caressed her mind, leading to a door concealing harsh memories. It was as if Roese was speaking to her from heaven.

Roese had been kidnapped a year back, and the abductors had returned her body in a casket. There was no incentive attached, they had made no demands, they had simply removed her sister off the face of the earth.

As much as Eliana missed her, there were times when her presence nearby felt more than a hallucination, and in world of magic, the possibility of the existence of spirits nd ghosts was too high for Eliana to set her thoughts aside.

Ganea was supposed to be her home, then why did it remind her of her worst nightmares?

"You look lost, Keizer," came Alexander's voice from where he sat across the table, cutting into his meat. Concern brimmed his black eyes where only darkness held fort.

"Three days..." she muttered, her voice shaking.

"You seemed rather excited to go. Have you changed your mind?" a tiny note of hopefulness crept into his voice as he asked that question.

"I am not sure, Alex. I just wish you could've come with me,"

A ghost of a smile appeared on his pale, pink lips. It held his expression as he replied in a small voice. "I wish I could've come with you too,"

Silence engulfed the table, her earlier fears wanning away.

There were different kinds of silences.

There was the silence before a brewing war, the silence before storm about to break free, the silence that existed between scholars as they read in the library, the awkward, uncomfortable silence, and so on, yet the kind Eliana experienced was a lover's silence, as peace stitched together the tattered pieces of her sanity and doubt and wrung it together.

The silence conveyed what perhaps words could never have.

"Alex?" she called his name as softly as she could, afraid of shattering the silence. It disappeared, yet the comfort and the sense of security lingered. His eyes lifted to meet hers, and she asked a simple meaningless question, "How does my hair look?" his eyes took in the white strand twisted and tied at the back with a simple robin clip and they lightened up at the sight of the pin.

"Dazzling, as always," his response set alight fire in her stomach and she felt her lips turn red at the compliment.

"I tried dying it, but the colour didn't stick," she confessed honestly, but that seemed to be the last thing on his mind. He eyed the almost full plate in front of her before pushing his chair back and gently ordering,

"Come here,"

Her legs worked of their own accordance as she rose and made her way towards the Prince. His arm slid around her waist as he pulled her closer and tilted his chin up to look at her in the eye. "That day, when you showed up in your lingerie, was a testimony to my self-control,"

Simple words that unravelled her, and quickened her breathing until she was close to panting with no movement, she chose to blame the cold wind for her hardened nipples.

The small movement didn't miss his eyes as a hearty laughter escaped his lips that were an inch from her body. "Eat first," he whispered, the hot exhale producing a sinful contrast against the coldness radiated by his immortal body.

Elian had only half-turned to grab a chair when he pulled her on his lap and settled her there, gripping her close. With his hand wrung around her waist, he clenched a knife and a fork with the other one. In a swift moment, he had a piece of meat raised against her mouth. "Open up, princess,"

Her lips parted on their own, and she couldn't lie for her life that the sudden salivation was caused by the smell of the meat. The heaving returned, but she snapped her teeth over the piece of meat before pulling it inside her mouth. She didn't mean for it to look seductive, yet heat crawled inside the Prince's eyes and his warning came in a low voice,

"Careful there, my little ribbon, you're playing with fire," She graced him with a coy smile and his grip tightened around her. "You need to eat, Eliana,"

"Why must I eat this," she started, her hand working to free the knife from his hand. He let her grasp it and she raised it to the side of his throat before continuing. "When I can have you, Your Highness?"

CHAPTER NINE

The first few days after the assault, Eliana had kept herself locked away from the world. The Queen visited from time to time to check in on her, guilt and concern etched on her face at Eliana's condition. The Prince had kept himself away, yet his involvement in the betterment of her condition was notable.

He gently pushed her towards art and then singing, kept her busy and his presence concealed. Her faith in her bracelet and his magic was the only component hindering her from tumbling into a life of fear. As long as it was around her wrist, she was certain he'd find her, she was certain he'd protect her.

He even asked his most trusted sentries to train her, to teach her how to fight.

He kept her from descending into darkness.

It took her a few months to heal completely, to push the trauma to the back of her mind and to stop having the nightmares on repeat, and that was when Alexander pulled back.

The only reminder of his existence was his daily visit to where she practiced her singing. It lingered and trailed her like a shadow, soothing her, comforting her in the oddest of the ways, yet piercing her soul apart as well.

They made appearances together in the public, sometimes sat beside each other during meals with potential allies and aquintances, and while he didn't downright ignore her, he made no effort to strengthen their bond.

Over the years, Eliana started to develop a small crush on him, yet every time it strted to blossom to something bigger, the Prince pushed her away, wordlessly reminding her that he never loved her.

The last of those instances, Eliana had spent weeks weaving a cloak for him and she'd gifted it to him on his birthday. The Prince had offered her a small 'thank you' before retiring to his chambers.

Four hours later, she'd witnessed a naked lady leave his chambers wrapped in nothing but that cloak, silently sneaking away. She'd found Eliana gaping at her, unshed tears in her eyes and had winked with a smirk before walking away, knowing well that she was Alex's betrothed.

In the morning, the cloak was in mud outside the castle's gate, and Eliana could only watch as wheels of carriages crushed it over and over again. She had come to bid the Prince goodbye for he was leaving to visit a nearby land. The Prince had offered her a small wave before his horse's hove had gotten stuck in the cloak and the Prince had demanded the guards in a cruel voice to get rid of the cloth.

It had taken her a week to nurse her broken heart, and when a guard had carried a message from the King, informing her that the Prince would return in three days, she had stormed to the Queen's chambers.

With the Queen's consent, she had departed to Deovalan Empire the morning of the Prince's arrival and as she passed the streets of Sleyisea, she prayed to the gods above that she wouldn't have to return back.

They had stopped at a manor belonging to one of the lords who was more than honored to let her and her guards stay.

She was given a beautiful golden room, with yellow light shinning and reflecting off the glassy architecture. It looked like a goddess's chamber at night. She had looked outside the balcony, glancing at the tall mountains guarding the eastern borders of Sleyisea, and a single tear had escaped her eyes.

She was about to fall asleep when a presence had filled the room, making her freeze. The lord had entered the room with a cruel lilt upon his smile. His brown hair was disheveled and madness covered his eyes entirely.

"The treaty has been destroying Sleyisea," he had started and she had backed away into a corner aware of the knife at her waist. "I have spent the last four years giving out free crops to sustain your damned land. No more..." the madness had disappeared for a mere second before the hunger had taken over.

Eliana had contemplated touching the bracelet around her wrists, but that would've, in a twisted way, meant that she was accepting her defeat, and her ego wouldn't have it.

Eliana had pressed her back tight against the solid wall at the sight of his eyes raking up and down her body and the long gown she wore. It covered almost everything, yet that didn't seam to displease him in the least.

"I was told to finish you off. Might as well take some advantage of you first,"

His fingers had curled to form a fist and invisible ropes had bound her limbs together. With a snap of his finger, all her clothes had vanished, leaving her bare in front of him. Her lips had been sealed shut by some power and he had grabbed one of her breasts before placing a sloppy kiss over her nipples and grabbing her rear.

She had tried to struggle, to fight him off and throw him away, but her body had been paralyzed the next moment. She had regretted not touching her bracelet when she could've when the bonds disappeared. She had tried to move even the slightest but the lord's magic had obstructed her from doing anything but breath.

He had pulled apart her legs and had lowered his pants. He had taken her hand and had rubbed it against his length while tears had streamed down her face. He would've penetrated had it not been for the banging on the doors.

"Turns out your guards are here," he and tsked his tongue before shaking his head and pulling his pants up. "Sorry, princess, but we're going to have to cut this short,"

With those words, he'd jabbed a knife straight into her chest.

Pain had exploded from that point to beyond, and she was certain she was going to die from it when a cool hand had come in contact with her forehead. The paralysis wore off and the pain vanished as grey eyes faced her and she felt a cloth against her wound.

"You're safe now, princess. No harm will befall you," the soothing words had left his lips and he had let her fall asleep in his arms. When she'd woken up, she was in a black room with floating flames. She hadn't needed anyone to tell her for her to know that they were the Prince's chambers.

The Prince sat on one of the velvet couch, his shoulders uptight and a blade drawn. His eyes were alert, for they turned to face her the moment she rose, leaking despair.

Pain tore through her chest making memories crash down on her. The blanket, which was at least four inches thick, suddenly felt too sheer. She took in his dilated pupils and wide eyes and felt tears drip down hers.

"Eliana, I am so sorry," he whispered, his voice hoarse. "Does it hurt too much?" Shame lingered in his voice, making a sob bleed through her lips.

"I am sorry," she cried. "I am so sorry," came her voice again. His expression transformed into a transfixed one at her words and he questioned,

"Whatever for?"

"Please don't send me back to Ganea. I never meant to bring down Sleyisea's honor. I-I'll behave in a better way. Please, I can't go back, my parents-"

"I am not sending you back to Ganea, Eliana," he spoke, his voice gentle and soothing, lacking it's natural icy edge. "Why would I-" he stopped himself as the realization dawned upon him. He pushed himself to his feet and reached her in three long strides, making her press herself against the frame of the bed.

The scene triggered her and she shut her eyes off again, her hand instinctively reaching for her bracelet. She felt the The Prince's movements halt and she partly opened her eyes to take a look at him. His gaze was furious, yet his tone remained soothing as his next words reached her,

"It's not your fault, Eliana. I would never ever blame you for what happened. *I* failed as your fiancé. You were entrusted to me, and I let you get hurt. *I* failed to protect you. Look at me, El," her eyes instantly found his and she asked,

"Did he- did he-" she broke down in another sob, unable to finish her sentence.

"No," he answered. "No, he didn't,"

Another sob, this one of relief and she gave him the smallest of the smiles. "You saved me. You saved me yet again!" flung her arms around him, conveying her gratitude through the tightness of the hug. "How-how did you know?" she asked him, pulling back.

"I came back and found you gone," he lowered his voice, and distress seeped from his next words. "I came with the intention of bringing you back home, or following you to wherever you went. I wasn't aware of what was happening, but I felt something tug at my heart, and something told me that you weren't alright. I broke the door to find a dagger in your chest.

I flung him away from you, had you taken away by the healers before torturing the assaulter until he gave up the name of the person who hired him for the job,"

He paused to look at her, to find her curiously glancing his way, waiting for him to say it. "Who was it?"

A single word broke through the night and her heart. "Estelle,"

She made a careful incision against the side of his throat and lowered his mouth to suck the blood of his neck. Her lips were about to come in contact with the warm liquid when Alexander wrapped a hand around her neck and pushed her away, shaking his head.

Her sole purpose behind the request was to get intoxicated, for she was aware she wouldn't be able to let the Prince hold her in any other way if she wasn't under some influence, like she was during their very first intimate night a few days back.

"If you don't want this, then we are not doing this," came the Prince's firm voice.

"I do want this, Alex," Her voice cracked, as she recalled what the memories did to her at times. The only way to suppress them was to consume alcohol or his blood or some certain herbs that she avoided.

She steered clear of the herbs, for they were known to leave behind profound effects, and since vampire blood provided faster intoxication, she was more inclined to consume it.

"I think I have something in mind that would work out without causing you discomfort or...inebriation," he paused, searching for something in her eyes, which he must've found, for he continued. "Come with me,"

He set her on her feet and she followed him to his bedroom, her footsteps faint as she contemplated the choice to run. It would've been easier, and it was a better option than engaging in an amorous congress with a vampire. The nervousness had her heart spiking, yet she was certain that the thrill played an important role in doing the same. To her surprise, instead of making his way to the bed, the Prince walked to the huge window covering a side of the room.

The curtains shielded them from the sparkling light spread across the city, yet Alexander clutched them and tore them away with a simple tug. "What are you doing?" Eliana questioned, gathering the curtains from his hands.

He didn't offer an explaination, and instead, walked over to a small cabinet by his bed. Kneeling down, he opened it to reveal a mass of thick ropes lying inside. Clutching them with one hand, he closed the door with another and walked back to where Eliana stood, baffled. She took a tentative step back, eying the ropes as if their mere touch was toxic.

"Relax, my little robin, they are not for you," To prove his words, Alex reached out the ropes to her, and she carefully curled her hand around the thick jute fibre as the weight of the words sank into her. "I shall help you tie me up, then,"

She considered it for a beat before dipping her head in the smallest of a nod. A dark smile crossed his face, causing her heart to pound rapidly into her ears.

He paced towards the windows and aimed a rope at the rod that was holding the curtains a few moments back. After doing the same with the other rope, he turned to face her, raising both of his hands.

She grabbed a chair, and pulled it towards him, the screech sending forbidden vibrations in her body. After climbing on it, she tied one of his hands with it before stepping down.

He brought his other hand to caress her cheek, but she clasped it and push it away before he could make contact. "Sh...you don't touch me until I ask you to," she whispered, lowering her voice to a seductive pitch. Sliding the chair over to the other side, she climbed on it and tied his other hand up as well.

She fisted his tunic, her breathes fast and shallow, before she began undoing the buttons. "I might have forgotten to mention this before, but you look exquisite, my dear prince," she spoke, eying his bare chest. His eyes met hers and something dark flickered in them that she was certain flickered in her eyes as well.

She gulped before pulling his pants down as well, revealing his length. The size made her gulp- from fear and anticipation at the same time. She stroked a finger against it, earning a hiss from him.

She smiled to herself in satisfaction before skipping out of her dress. The corset fit her perfectly, providing teasing glimpses of her breast. Her fingers fiddled with the straps as she slowly undid the knot and pulled herself out the corset, leaving her in a chemise.

Placing her palm flat against his chest, she raised to her tiptoes and pressed a soft kiss against his lips before withdrawing completely. She pulled the chemise over her head, leaving her bare apart from her underwear.

His jaw visibly clenched and she began kissing his neck and made her way down to her chest. Her one hand gripped his hair while the other lowered to give another stroke to his hardness.

Her kisses lowered from his chest to her naval before she reached his length. She swallowed once before pressing a peck against it, recounting the things the female protagonists did in those romance novels when they made love to their partners.

She wrapped her fingers around him, pumping once, twice, and thrice, before letting go of him. She could mark the way he strained against the ropes he could've broken if he wanted, and the way his veins popped as he tried to contain himself.

She knelt before him, trembling slightly as she performed a ritual completely foreign to her. She grabbed a hold of her breasts before pressing him in the center of her chest right between her breasts. She pushed them together, squeezing his length, making him groan softly.

She pushed them up and down, over and over again until his release came, spraying her all over her chest, the white dripping down till her naval.

She felt her own juices drip down her thighs and she skimmed out of her underwear before lying down in front of him, spreading her legs wide for him to have a clear view of her heat from above.

The floor was cold under her back, a contrast to her suddenly hot body. She adjusted herself before bending her knees and pressing her heels against the floor.

Her fingers toyed with her nipples before she reached out a hand to stroke her heat. Circling it, she looking at the Prince in the eye, only to find his gaze all over her body. She pressed a finger against her clit, and found herself coming in a matter of minutes, she found herself moaning a release.

"Eliana," the Prince growled warningly and she discovered pure lust in his eyes due to her performance. She offered him a small sadistic smile, one she never knew she had in herself, before kneeling back in front of him. This time, she gathered the courage to take him in her mouth and began sucking, softly and first and then in a quick-paced manner before taking him all inside, triggering a gag reflex.

He thrusted against her, pushing in and out, before she began dark spot in her eyes from lust and the lack of oxygen. When he came, she made certain to swallow every last bit, for a second forgetting her title, and acting like a starved madwoman.

She crumbled to the floor right after, her chest heaving with exhaustion at the intimate activity, before she managed to pull herself to her feet. The Prince must've seen the timidness in her eyes for his softened and the ropes slowly undid themselves and he cupped her cheeks with his hands before placing a tender kiss against the center of her, where the scar from years back rested.

"A hot bath?" he suggested and she nodded, pressing a hand against her mouth when a yawn tried to escape it. He gave her a smile that for once, touched his eyes and her very soul as well before he lifted her off the ground and walked to the bath with her.

She rested her head against his chest, enjoying the cold skin as he walked in silence. Her lips curled as his actions touched her soul- not only the bath, but the way he let her tie him up so she won't feel the fear, and how he saved her every time.

She suddenly felt very grateful for being married off to a man like him, and for a few moments, the bliss covered anything ill he may have done in the past.

CHAPTER TEN

Eliana had spent the rest of the week in the Prince's chambers where he had watched over her through the day and the entire night. She had asked the Prince whether he slept at all and he had replied, 'Sometimes', but when she had offered to sleep back in her room so he could sleep on his bed, he had turned it down in the beat of a heart.

Eliana had never dared to ask more about Estelle, for she knew it was of no use. Estelle was the Queen of Sleyisea, and while she had tried to kill Eliana, she was certain that she would face no consequences for her actions.

Yet on the 6th night of their stay together, Alexander had wandered into a room, had served her a hot meal in the bed prior to telling her that Estelle was being hanged the day after for treason.

According to him, Estella had tried to break the treaty between Ganea and Sleyisea by attempting to kill her, which was a crime not only against her, but against Sleyisea as well. The thought scared Eliana. Whether or not Estelle had tried to get her murdered, she had been a reliable and sweet companion towards her for years.

While her mood had dampened further, she hadn't failed to notice the grimness on Alexander's face. "Are you quite alright?" she had asked him and he had looked her straight in the eye, the sharp grey coldness seeping deep inside her soul.

"I am," he had asked, but the roughness in his tone hadn't matched his reassurance and she had pushed her food aside along with her plate, clearing her lap.

"Lie down," she'd offered him in a small, consoling voice, making him shoot her a glare. She would've been afraid, if she hadn't known that he wouldn't kill her. That was treason, right? "My sister used to let me sleep in her lap whenever I was upset. It used to calm me down,"

He had given her a stare before curling himself so he fit on the small portion of the bed and resting his head on her lap with a sigh. His shoulders had slumped, and she had been able to see the exhaustion and the wariness in his shoulder as he had lied there.

She had immediately put a hand on his head, sliding fingers through it in gentle motions. His wild silver eyes had shut themselves after a while, and she felt immensely proud of herself for being able to relax the vampire.

"I am sorry for what these eyes had to see, for what this body had to bear and for what these lips had to supress," he had whispered, making her eyes swell up with tears. "Marry me, Eliana?" the question had been sincere, and the brokenness in his voice had been palpable.

She had nodded frantically before continuing her tiny scalp massage.

"The dress has arrived," he had informed her, his voice low. "The wedding's day after tomorrow,"

Eliana had to watch one of her previously favourite persons get hanged. Estelle had met her eye once, remorse shinning on her face brighter than the spring sun, before her face had been covered by the black cloth bag and the floor under her had given out.

Eliana hadn't been able to watch it and had casted her eyes done as the fallen Queen had drawn her final breathes.

Alexander had held her hand through it all despite himself looking tense.

"I am so sorry," she had whispered with tears sliding down her tears. He had wiped them away before asking her,

"What for, my little robin?"

"You must've been close to her. She's dead because of me,"

Prince Thaddeus, who had been sitting next Alexander, had shot them an apprehensive look, presumably after hearing her words.

"She got what she deserved, Eliana," he had answered, his voice hard. Eliana had gulped before being escorted back to the Prince's chambers by the guards.

He hadn't returned to his chambers that night. Eliana had waited till two in the morning, after which, she had gone back to sleep in her own bed. Some time during the night, the door to her chambers had opened, and she could vaguely remembered making out the Prince's figure before letting the sleep take her again.

When she had woken up in the morning, she hadn't found Alex by her side. Instead, she had found maids gushing over her, giggling, as they took in her wedding dress. She had been taken back by the dress as well. It was a supposedly simple looking dress with a sweetheart neckline and drooping sleeves make of loosely stitched net. The skirt had a layer of net over the silk which was embroided with white flowers and roses.

The maids had helped her draw a bath and she had found her heart pacing rapidly with blooming anxiety. Her last day as a married woman, and while she had very much anticipated it, everything had suddenly started to feel too surreal.

The maids had pulled her out of the bath and had given her rose-scented steam to infuse the scent in her skin. After that, they had proceeded to paint her face before helping her into the enormous gown.

Needless to say, it had fit her perfectly.

They had curled her hair and had let it spring down naturally against her shoulders before sliding the perfect pair of heels over her feet.

Princess Auriol had been waiting for Eliana at her door and had helped her walk down to the hall where the ceremony was to take place. The place had been crowded with thousands of people, all eagerly waiting to see their Prince wed for the first time in five hundred years.

Roese hadn't been able to make it on the short notice, so, Eliana had no one but Prince Thaddeus to walk her down the aisle to where Alexander stood, a spec of nervousness evident on his face as well. She had offered him the smallest of the smiles before standing right in front of him as the priest had commenced the ceremony.

Eliana's mind had gone blank until the priest had spoken, "You may kiss the bride,"

Eliana's heart rate had touched the very gates of heaven, and the Prince must've sensed it, for he did lean down but it was to only place a kiss against her forehead. Some people had cheered while some had cooed but their voices had synced into a gasp as the white of her gown had morphed slowly into crimson.

Someone had spelled it or it was blessing from the gods, Eliana knew not, yet it had made her smile.

They had danced later, an unchoreographed performance that had looked more refined than it possible could've, before the Prince had pulled her upstairs, back inside his chambers.

"You know, last night, when I returned and I didn't find you in here..." he had begun after closing the door behind them, his eyes focused towards the floor. "For a second, I was so afraid, my little robin,"

"I am sorry-"

"No, it's not your doing. I had brought that upon myself, and I cannot convey how ashamed I am for that. You have my sincerest apologies for that, Eliana,"

Eliana had offered him a bright smile before pulling him into a hug. "You have been too kind to me, Alexander. I am grateful for that,"

"Now, come on, my little robin, you look like you could use a bath. Your clothes are in there, go freshen up!"

When Eliana had returned, she had found Alexander lying on the couch with his eyes sealed. She was aware that he had been asleep, and had only been pretending to spare her from being afraid or embarrassed. She hadn't called him out on it, and had simply raised his head before sliding a pillow under it.

A hint of a smile had played out on his lips at the gesture, yet he hadn't broken his act completely, and Eliana had felt grateful to all the gods above for giving her the loving husband they had.

Eliana found herself staring at a distance in the night sky, taking in the moon's glorious light, reminiscing how she'd felt so safe around him.

"You shouldn't be standing here right now," she heard his voice from behind her, causing her to turn around to face him. She found him standing with his tunic missing, exposing his bare chest to the pale white glint emerging from beneath the clouds.

"Why not, my Prince?" she asked, picking up on his playful tone.

"Because you look so gorgeous when the moonlight's hitting you, it frightens me that somebody is going to whisk you away," he whispered in response, and she felt blood rush to her cheeks.

"No one's ever going to whisk me away, Alex," she responded softly, her voice carried by the winds over to his ears and his only. "Till death do us apart, remember?" he leaned forward to place a kiss against her lips before saying, "Not even death. To where you go, I'll follow. And to whichever hellhole I sink, I'll take you,"

He turned her around so her back was pressed against his front as they took in the fresh humid air of the nearing dawn.

"The moon is so beautiful, isn't it?"

"Yes," she replied, tilting her head slightly to look him in the eye. "Yes, it is,"

Last day preparations for Ganea had taken a toll on Eliana's body, especially her head, which had started aching in the early hours after sunrise. She was to leave the following day, yet her head did not seem to take a hint and stay strong for even five minutes straight.

She barely managed to make it through the day and once she was done, she decided to visit Alexander's room to spend as much time with him as she could. When she entered, she found the room empty of any soul, and could only guess Alex's whereabouts.

Deciding to wait, she slipping out of her heels and lied on his bed, staring at the star-like projections on his ceilings. Many-a-nights, she had let herself fall asleep by merely gazing into them when she was thirteen, their distant warmth soothing her.

A heap of ropes on the floor caught her eye. She could only assume that they were from their night from two days back. The memories solely were enough to make her fluster at the newfound courage she'd gained at that moment.

She let herself slither down the silk sheets of the Prince's bed before walking up to where the ropes lay. She knelt down and gathered the jute in her lap, smiling at herself at how they then smelled equally of the Prince and the fabric.

She eyes the cabinet from where the Prince had produced them before making a quick decision to put them back inside it. She opened the cabinet's door to be greeted by a stack of what looked like letters.

She set them aside before carefully putting the ropes inside. She picked up the letters and just as she was going to place them inside as well, she noticed the name of the sender.

Roese.

Her heart stopped for a moment before she recollected herself and checked the date of the letter. It had been sent a mere week before Roese had died. Elian noticed that they were all arranged in the order of when they were sent and she quickly pulled out the first letter.

Dear Prince Alexander of Sleyisea,

I wish I could've met you before my parents agreed to letting you marry my sister, Eliana. I wish so, because then, firstly, I would've known what sort of man you were, and secondly, you would've known the amount of danger you would be in if you were to ever hurt my sister.

On that note, despite how much I would hate to scare you or start our brother-sister relationship this way, I must warn you that if my sister shed as much as a tear because of you, I will slid a knife through your immortal heart and perhaps carve it out if that is what kills you.

I hope you have a good day ahead,

Also, congratulations on the engagement,

Princess Roise.

Eliana found tears pricking the corner of her eyes at the fierce protectiveness of her sister and guilt consumed her completely as she realized how it hadn't crossed her mind even once to threaten Roese's husband.

Pushing it aside, she pulled out the second letter and began reading.

Dear Prince Alexander,

The circumstances you are in are quite weird, if I am being frank, however, now, I am certain that you will not let any harm come to her.

However, my concern now is her age. She is barely nine, so I hope you keep your claws off her for the next few years: a decade would be good, but at least until she is sixteen. She is too young and the last thing I want is for her to be traumatized.

Princess Roese

Eliana wasn't certain what circumstances Roese was speaking of, yet she pushed them to the back of her mind before grabbing the second to the last letter, trying to know as much as she could before Alex were to come.

Alexxxxx,

Gods, have I told you I am going to be a mom?

And have I told you I am going to be a mom??

I cannot believe this! I wasn't certain until a few weeks back and then my devil of a husband (more like my hottest prince charming) didn't let me tell anyone in the fear of this news falling into the wrong hands, but now that I am showing, there's no use hiding it anyway!

You better let my sister come visit me, and you can come as well if you want, though I would wait a few months until I get less hormonal or I might throw you off the balcony for as much as holding El's hand.

Anyways, I am hoping to see you soon.

Your favourite sister-in-law,

What? You need me to write a name here? How dare you, mister? How many girls have you promised the title of 'favourite sister-in-law to'?

Eliana chuckled quietly at her sister's antics. She had always been dramatic and braver than Eliana could've ever been.

She hadn't failed to notice how her letter had been friendly, as if she and Alex had slowly become friends, and guilt clawed up again, reminding her how she'd not once shared a correspondence with Daniel, Roese's husband.

She pulled out the last letter and read.

Alex,

It's a boy, it's a boy, IT'S A BOY!

Thank you so much for agreeing to visit! I am very grateful towards you for that! I cannot wait to meet you and my sister.

Coming back to my baby boy...

We have decided to name him Anthony after some dead grandfather of Daniel. I am not very close to him, but I know he meant a lot to Daniel, so here we are. I honestly believe that naming kids after dead people is very creepy, but it made Daniel happy, and there's little I wouldn't do for him, but I think you what that feels like, with Eliana being your mate and all.

Anyways, so, I asked Daniel to talk about the routes with you-

Eliana paused reading for a moment, drew in a shaky breath before reading the last two lines again.

but I think you what that feels like, with Eliana being your mate and all.

with Eliana being your mate and all.
Eliana being your mate and all.
Eliana being your mate.
Mate.

Eliana screamed on the inside yet only a mere whimper escaped her lips. Alexander had known that she was her mate, and perhaps that was why he had chosen to marry her, but if she was indeed his mate...

Why choose so many other girls one after the other?

A sob wrecked through her body, the memories of naked girls leaving his bedroom cutting deeper now that she knew that he was her mate. Men mistreated their wives by bringing over whores and mistresses, but their mates? Never.

The door opened behind her but she didn't bother to turn. She pulled herself to her feet that were shaking slightly from rage or sadness, she knew not.

"You're my mate..." she whispered, barely keeping herself in check. His eyes widened slightly, but he managed to contain his surprise and hold his poker face. "I am your mate..."

"Well, yes," he spoke, snatching the last letter that was between her fingers.

"How come you never told me?"

"It wasn't important," he answered, and his words shattered her heart.

It wasn't important. The words echoed in her ears as she pushed him aside and left his room, leaving the door open in case he wanted to pursue her. She waited for the hours to come, but he never came.

Not once, not when she laid sobbing on her bed or when the guards lifted her trunks downstairs and when she walked down the stairs of the castle, away to the carriage that awaited her.

She hugged the Queen goodbye before dipping into a curtsy before the King who pulled her up and into his arms. He wiped away the treacherous tears that were making their way down her cheeks before pressing a kiss against her forehead.

"Come home soon," he told her, a smile gracing his face.

Home. His words reminded her that Sleyisea was her home, not Ganea.

She manged to nod before her gaze shifted to a wing of the castle, the one which bore the Prince's room.

The King followed her line of vision before speaking softly, "He cannot see you leave, Eliana,"

She again gave him a shaky nod before dipping into another curtsy and turning around and taking a seat inside the carriage. She waved at the King and the Queen, taking in their sight and the castle one last time before a guard closed the door of the carriage.

Only then did she lean her back against the cushiony back-support of the carriage, waiting for the Prince to come to apologise, to stop her, but no prayer of hers was answered.

The people of Sleyisea waved at her and they had to stop every few hundred metres as they gifted her things. It was a tradition in Sleyisea. Every time a princess-consort or a queen-consort went to visit her homeland, she was drowned in gifts by the people of Sleyisea to remind her that she was loved, to give her a reason to come back.

They were nearing the border of the city when they stopped yet again. For a land known for its ruthless beasts, Sleyisea had warm and loving people. She was presented with another heap of clothes, flowers, jewellery, and pieces of art.

Women, men and children, all came to toss their gifts, and to give her their blessings. The crones kissed her on the cheeks or on the forehead, while she did so with the younger children.

A man, dressing in all black in a way suspiciously close to that of a warrior, face covered by a black cloth and a hood pulled over his head, came her way, tossed something at her feet before disappearing.

Curiously, Eliana bent to pick it, only to find a ring, and not just any ring. It had a red diamond atop with the most beautiful of carvings of gold around it. It was her first engagement ring, the one Alexander had slipped over her finger during the ceremony.

She'd outgrown it and had stopped wearing it after Alexander had another ring forged for her, yet there it was, looking the same way before, and if it hadn't been for the blazing torches, she would have never noticed the only difference as she rolled it between her fingers.

On the inside of the band, there was a word engraved.

Alexander.

Moonlit Vows

Ganea was far from the land Eliana remembered leaving behind. The moment her carriage crossed the borders, Eliana felt the air thicken, and a wave of unrecognisable and unseeable gas entered her lungs, confiscating all the air.

The soldiers around her felt it too, for they wheezed alongside her before signalling the coachman to stop the carriage, and the others followed the suit. The carriages came to a halt, and all the mercenaries, even the most skilled ones, dropped to their knees clutching their chests as the poisonous airs filtered their capillaries and diffused inside their arteries.

"Retreat back!" a soldier managed to shout over sounds of men struggling and dying. A bulkier soldier managed to pull Eliana out of the carriage and lifted her in his arms before pulling her out of the carriage. He made a run for the border, desperate to reach the other side, back to Sleyisea.

But they were too far away, a hundred metres across the border, and the soldier fell to his knees before they were halfway there, and Eliana collapsed alongside him.

She almost reached for her bracelet, almost instinctively grasped it before remembering the treaty and the fact that she was in Ganean territory and the consequences Alexander would have to face if, by any chance, they were to get caught.

Around her, she could see the soldiers passing away and she felt her own consciousness slip away. She clasped her hand around her neck, a sole person on her mind as she drifted in and out before diving in finally.

VENTURES OF GEM LAND
The Black Time
JANUSHI RAICHURA

VENTURES OF GEM LAND
The Gorgon's Curse
JANUSHI RAICHURA

VENTURES OF GEM LAND

The Alchemic Presage

JANUSHI RAICHURA

VENTURES OF GEM LAND

The Banished Heretics